THE DANCE OF DEATH

THE DANCE
OF DEATH

AND OTHER STORIES

ALGERNON BLACKWOOD

PAN BOOKS LTD : LONDON

First published 1927 by Herbert Jenkins Ltd.
This edition published 1963 by Pan Books Ltd.,
33 Tothill Street, London, S.W.1

ISBN 0 330 01645 8

2nd Printing 1973

PRINTED AND BOUND IN ENGLAND BY
HAZELL WATSON AND VINEY LTD
AYLESBURY, BUCKS

CONTENTS

The Dance of Death

Browne went to the dance feeling genuinely depressed, for the doctor had just warned him that his heart was weak and that he must be exceedingly careful in the matter of exertion.

'Dancing?' he asked, with that assumed lightness some natures affect in the face of a severe shock – the plucky instinct to conceal pain.

'Well – in moderation, perhaps,' hummed the doctor. 'Not *wildly*!' he added, with a smile that betrayed something more than mere professional sympathy.

At any other time Browne would probably have laughed, but the doctor's serious manner put a touch of ice on the springs of laughter. At the age of twenty-six one hardly realises death; life is still endless; and it is only old people who have 'hearts' and such-like afflictions. So it was that the professional dictum came as a real shock; and with it too, as a sudden revelation, came that little widening of sympathy for others that is part of every deep experience as the years roll up and pass.

At first he thought of sending an excuse. He went about carefully, making the buses stop dead before he got out, and going very slowly up steps. Then gradually he grew more accustomed to the burden of his dread secret: the commonplace events of the day; the hated drudgery of the office, where he was an underpaid clerk; the contact with other men who bore similar afflictions with assumed indifference; the fault-finding of the manager, making him fearful of his position – all this helped to reduce the sense of first alarm, and, instead of sending an excuse, he went to the dance, as we have seen, feeling deeply depressed, and moving all the time as if he carried in his side a brittle glass globe that the least jarring might break into a thousand pieces.

The spontaneous jollity natural to a boy and girl dance served, however, to emphasise vividly the contrast of his own mood, and to make him very conscious again of his little hidden source of pain. But, though he would gladly have availed himself of a sympathetic ear among the many there whom he knew intimately, he nevertheless exercised the restraint natural to his character, and avoided any reference to the matter that bulked so largely in his consciousness. Once or twice he was tempted, but a prevision of the probable conversation that would ensue stopped him always in time: 'Oh, I *am* so sorry, Mr Browne, and you mustn't dance *too* hard, you know,' and then his careless laugh as he remarked that it didn't matter a bit, and his little joke as he whirled his partner off for another spin.

He knew, of course, that there was nothing very sensational about being told that one's heart was weak. Even the doctor had smiled a little; and he now recalled more than one acquaintance who had the same trouble and made light of it. Yet it sounded in Browne's life a note of profound and sinister gloom. It snatched beyond his reach at one fell swoop all that he most loved and enjoyed, destroying a thousand dreams, and painting the future a dull drab colour without hope. He was an idealist at heart, hating the sordid routine of the life he led as a business underling. His dreams were of the open air, of mountains, forests, and great plains, of the sea, and of the lonely places of the world. Wind and rain spoke intimately to his soul, and the storms of heaven, as he heard them raging at night round his high room in Bloomsbury, stirred savage yearnings that haunted him for days afterwards with the voices of the desert. Sometimes during the lunch hour, when he escaped temporarily from the artificial light and close air of his high office stool, to see the white clouds sailing by overhead, and to hear the wind singing in the wires, it set such a fever in his blood that for the remainder of the afternoon he found it impossible to concentrate on his work, and thus exasperated the loud-voiced manager almost to madness.

Having no expectations, and absolutely no practical business ability, he was fortunate, however, in having a 'place' at all, and the hard fact that promotion was unlikely made him all the more careful to keep his dreams in their place, to do his work as well as possible, and to save what little he could.

His holidays were the only points of light in an otherwise dreary existence. And one day, when he should have saved enough, he looked forward vaguely to a life close to Nature, perhaps a shepherd on a hundred hills, a dweller in the woods, within sound of his beloved trees and waters, where the smell of the earth and camp-fire would be ever in his nostrils, and the running stream always ready to bear his boat swiftly away into happiness.

And now the knowledge that he had a weak heart came to spoil everything. It shook his dream to the very foundations. It depressed him utterly. Any moment the blow might fall. It might catch him in the water, swimming, or half-way up the mountain, or midway in one of his lonely tramps, just when his enjoyment depended most upon his being reckless and forgetful of bodily limitations – that freedom of the spirit in the wilderness he so loved. He might even be forced to spend his holiday, to say nothing of the dream of the far future, in some farmhouse '*quietly*,' instead of gloriously in the untrodden wilds. The thought made him angry with pain. All day he was haunted and dismayed, and all day he heard the wind whispering among branches and the water lapping somewhere against sandy banks in the sun.

The dance was a small subscription affair, hastily arranged and happily informal. It took place in a large hall that was used in the daytime as a gymnasium, but the floor was good and the music more than good. Foils and helmets hung round the walls, and high up under the brown rafters were ropes, rings, and trapezes coiled away out of reach, their unsightliness further concealed by an array of brightly coloured flags. Only the light was not of the best, for the hall was very long, and the gallery at the far end loomed in a sort of twilight that was further deepened by the shadows of the flags overhead. But its benches afforded excellent sitting-out places, where strong light was not always an essential to happiness, and no one dreamed of finding fault.

At first he danced cautiously, but by degrees the spirit of

the time and place relieved his depression and helped him to forget. He had probably exaggerated the importance of his malady. Lots of other fellows, even as young as he was, had weak hearts and thought nothing of it. All the time, however, there was an undercurrent of sadness and disappointment not to be denied. Something had gone out of life. A note of darkness had crept in. He found his partners dull, and they no doubt found him still duller.

Yet this dance, with nothing apparently to distinguish it from a hundred others, stood out in all his experience with an indelible red mark against it. It is a common trick of Nature – and a profoundly significant one – that, just when despair is deepest, she waves a wand before the weary eyes and does her best to waken an impossible hope. Her idea, presumably, being to keep her victim going actively to the very end of the chapter, lest through indifference he should lose something of the lesson she wishes to teach.

Thus it was that, midway in the dance, Browne's listless glance fell upon a certain girl whose appearance instantly galvanised him into a state of keenest possible desire. A flash of white light entered his heart and set him all on fire to know her. She attracted him tremendously. She was dressed in pale green, and always danced with the same man – a man about his own height and colouring, whose face, however, he never could properly see. They sat out together much of the time – always in the gallery where the shadows were deepest. The girl's face he saw clearly, and there was something about her that simply lifted him bodily out of himself and sent strange thrills of delight coursing over him like shocks of electricity. Several times their eyes met, and when this happened he could not tear his glance away. She fascinated him, and all the forces in his being merged into a single desire to be with her, to dance with her, speak with her, and to know her name. Especially he wondered who the man was she so favoured; he reminded him so oddly of himself. No one knows precisely what he himself looks like, but this tall dark figure, whose face he never could contrive to see, started the strange thought in him that it was his own *double*.

In vain he sought to compass an introduction to this girl.

No one seemed to know her. Her dress, her hair, and a certain wondrous slim grace made him think of a young tree waving in the wind; of ivy leaves; of something that belonged to the life of the woods rather than to ordinary humanity. She possessed him, filling his thoughts with wild woodland dreams. Once, too, he was certain when their eyes met that she smiled at him, and the call was so wellnigh irresistible that he almost dropped his partner's arm to run after her.

But it seemed impossible to obtain an introduction from anyone.

'Do you know who that girl is over there?' he asked one of his partners while sitting out a square dance, half exhausted with his exertions; 'the one up there in the gallery?'

'In pink?'

'No, the one in green, I mean.'

'Oh, next the wall-flower lady in red!'

'*In* the gallery, not *under* it,' he explained impatiently.

'I can't see up there. It's so dark,' returned the girl after a careful survey through glasses. 'I don't think I see any one at all.'

'It *is* rather dark,' he remarked.

'Why? Do you know who she is?' she asked foolishly.

He did not like to insist. It seemed so rude to his partner. But this sort of thing happened once or twice. Evidently no one knew this girl in green, or else he described her so inaccurately that the people he asked looked at someone else instead.

'In that green sort of ivy-looking dress,' he tried another.

'With the rose in her hair and the red nose? Or the one sitting out?'

After that he gave it up finally. His partners seemed to sniff a little when he asked. Evidently *la désirée* was not a popular maiden. Soon after, too, she disappeared and he lost sight of her. Yet the thought that she might have gone home made his heart sink into a sort of horrible blackness.

He lingered on much later than he intended in the hope of getting an introduction, but at last, when he had filled all his engagements, or nearly all, he made up his mind to slip out and go home. It was already late, and he had to be in the office – that hateful office – punctually at nine o'clock. He felt tired, awfully tired, more so than ever before at a dance. It was, of course, his weak heart. He still dawdled a little while, however, hoping for another glimpse of the sylph in green, hungering for a last look that he could carry home with him and perhaps mingle with his dreams. The mere thought of her filled him with pain and joy, and a sort of rarefied delight he had never known before. But he could not wait for ever, and it was already close upon two o'clock in the morning. His rooms were only a short distance down the street; he would light a cigarette and stroll home. No; he had forgotten for a moment; *without* a cigarette: the doctor had been very stern on that point.

He was in the act of turning his back on the whirl of dancing figures, when the flags at the far end of the room parted for an instant in the moving air, and his eye rested upon the gallery just visible among the shadows.

A great pain ran swiftly through his heart as he looked. There were only two figures seated there: the tall dark man, who was his double, and the ivy girl in green. She was looking straight at him down the length of the room, and even at that distance he could see that she smiled.

He stopped short. The flags waved back again and hid the picture, but on the instant he made up his mind to act. There, among all this dreary crowd of dancing dolls, was someone he really wanted to know, to speak with, to touch – someone who drew him beyond all he had ever known, and made his soul cry aloud. The room was filled with automatic lay-figures, but here was someone *alive*. He must know her. It was impossible to go home without speech, utterly impossible.

A fresh stab of pain, worse than the first, gave him momentary pause. He leant against the wall for an instant just under the clock, where the hands pointed to two, waiting for the swooning blackness to go. Then he passed on, disregarding it utterly. It supplied him, in truth, with the extra little impetus he needed to set the will into vigorous action, for it reminded him forcibly of what *might* happen. His time might be short; he had known few enough of the good things of life; he would seize what he could. He had no introduction, but — to the devil with the conventions. The risk was nothing. To meet her eyes at close quarters, to hear her voice, to know something of the perfume of that hair and dress — what was the risk of a snub compared to that?

He slid down the side of the long room, dodging the dancers as best he could. The tall man, he noted, had left the gallery, but the girl sat on alone. He made his way quickly up the wooden steps, light as air, trembling with anticipation. His heart beat like a quick padded hammer, and the blood played a tambourine in his ears. It was odd he did not meet the tall man on the stairs, but doubtless there was another exit from the gallery that he had not observed. He topped the stairs and turned the corner. By Jove, she was still there, a few feet in front of him, sitting with her arms upon the railing, peering down upon the dancers below. His eyes swam for a moment, and something clutched at the very roots of his being.

But he did not hesitate. He went up quite close past the empty seats, meaning to ask naturally and simply if he might beg for the pleasure of a dance. Then, when he was within a few feet of her side, the girl suddenly turned and faced him, and the words died away on his lips. They seemed absolutely foolish and inadequate.

'Yes, I am ready,' she said quietly, looking straight into his eyes; 'but what a long time you were in coming. Was it such a great effort to leave?'

The form of the question struck him as odd, but he was too happy to pause. He became transfigured with joy. The sound of her voice instantly drowned all the clatter of the ballroom, and seemed to him the only thing in the whole world. It did not break on the consonants like most human speech. It flowed smoothly; it was the sound of wind among branches, of water running over pebbles. It swept into him and caught him away, so that for a moment he saw his beloved woods and hills and seas. The stars were somewhere in it too, and the murmur of the plains.

By the gods! Here was a girl he could speak with in the words of silence; she stretched every string in his soul and then played on them. His spirit expanded with life and happiness. She would listen gladly to all that concerned him. To her he could talk openly about his poor broken heart, for she would sympathise. Indeed, it was all he could do to prevent himself running forward at once with his arms outstretched to take her. There was a perfume of earth and woods about her.

'Oh, I am so *awfully* glad —' he began lamely, his eyes on her face. Then, remembering something of earthly manners, he added:

'My name – er – is —'

Something unusual – something indescribable – in her gesture stopped him. She had moved to give him space at her side.

'Your name!' she laughed, drawing her green skirts with a soft rustle like leaves along the bench to make room; 'but you need no name *now*, you know!'

Oh, the wonder of it! She understood him. He sat down with a feeling that he had been flying in a free wind and was resting among the tops of trees. The room faded out temporarily.

'But my name, if you like to know, is Issidy," she said, still smiling.

'Miss Issidy,' he stammered, making another attempt at the forms of worldly politeness.

'Not *Miss* Issidy,' she laughed aloud merrily. It surely was the sound of wind in poplars. 'Issidy is my first name; so if you call me anything, you must call me that.'

The name was pure music in his ears, but though he blundered about in his memory to find his own, it had utterly vanished; for the life of him he could not recollect what his friends called him. He stared a moment, vaguely wondering, almost beside himself with delight. No other girls he had known – ye heavens above! there were no longer any other girls! He had never known any other girl than this one. Here was his universe, framed in a green dress, with a voice of sea and wind, eyes like the sun, and movements of bending grasses. All else was mere shadow and fantasy. For the first time in his existence he was alive, and knew that he was alive.

'I was sure you would come to me,' she was saying. 'You

couldn't help yourself.' Her eyes were always on his face.

'I was afraid at first —'

'But your thoughts,' she interrupted softly, 'your thoughts were up here with me all the time.'

'You knew that!' he cried, delighted.

'I felt them,' she replied simply. 'They — you kept me company, for I have been alone here all the evening. I know no one else here – *yet*.'

Her words amazed him. He was just going to ask who the tall dark man was, when he saw that she was rising to her feet and that she wanted to dance.

'But my heart —' he stammered.

'It won't hurt your poor heart to dance with *me*, you know,' she laughed. 'You may trust me. I shall know how to take care of it.'

Browne felt simply ecstatic; it was too wonderful to be true; it was impossible – this meeting in London, at an ordinary dull dance, in the twentieth century. He would wake up presently from a dream of silver and gold. Yet he felt even then that she was drawing his arm about her waist for the dance, and with that first magical touch he almost lost consciousness and passed with her into a state of pure spirit.

It puzzled him for a moment how they reached the floor so quickly and found themselves among the whirling couples. He had no recollection of coming down the stairs. But meanwhile he was dancing on wings, and the girl in green beside him seemed to fly too, and as he pressed her to his heart he found it impossible to think of anything else in the world but that – that and his astounding happiness.

And the music was within them, rather than without; indeed they seemed to make their own music out of their swift whirling movements, for it never ceased and he never grew tired. His heart had ceased to pain him. Other curious things happened, too, but he hardly noticed them; or, rather, they no longer seemed strange. In that crowded ballroom they never once touched other people. His partner required no steering. She made no sound. Then suddenly he realised that his own feet made no sound either. They skimmed the floor with noiseless feet like spirits dancing. No one else appeared to take the least notice of them. Most of the faces seemed, indeed, strange to him now, as though he had not seen them before, but once or twice he could have sworn that he passed couples who were dancing almost as happily and lightly as themselves, couples he had known in past years, couples who were dead.

Gradually the room emptied of its original comers, and others filled their places, silently, with airy graceful movements and happy faces, till the whole floor at length was covered with the soundless feet and whirling forms of those who had already left the world. And, as the artificial light faded away, there came in its place a soft white light that filled the room with beauty and made all the faces look radiant. And, once, as they skimmed past a mirror, he saw that the girl beside him was not there -- that he seemed to be dancing alone, clasping no one; yet when he glanced down, there was her magical face at his shoulder and he felt her little form pressing up against him.

Such dancing, too, he had never even dreamed about, for it was like swinging with the tree-tops in the winds.

Then they danced farther out, ever swifter and swifter, past the shadows beneath the gallery, under the motionless hanging flags – and out into the night. The walls were behind them. They were off their feet and the wind was in their hair. They were rising, rising, rising towards the stars.

He felt the cool air of the open sky on his cheeks, and when he looked down, as they cleared the summit of the dark-lying hills, he saw that Issidy had melted away into himself and they had become one being. And he knew then that his heart would never pain him again on earth, or cause him to fear for any of his beloved dreams.

*   *   *

But the manager of the 'hateful office' only knew two days later why Browne had not turned up to his desk, nor sent any word to explain his absence. He read it in the paper – how he had dropped down dead at a dance, suddenly stricken by heart disease. It happened just before two o'clock in the morning.

'Well,' thought the manager, 'he's no loss to us, anyhow. He had no real business instincts. Smith will do his work much better—and for less money, too.'

A Psychical Invasion

'AND WHAT is it makes you think I could be of use in this particular case?' asked Dr John Silence, looking across somewhat sceptically at the Swedish lady in the chair facing him.

'Your sympathetic heart and your knowledge of occultism —'

'Oh, please – that dreadful word!' he interrupted, holding up a finger with a gesture of impatience.

'Well, then,' she laughed, 'your wonderful clairvoyant gift and your trained psychic knowledge of the processes by which a personality may be disintegrated and destroyed – these strange studies you've been experimenting with all these years —'

'If it's only a case of multiple personality I must really cry off,' interrupted the doctor again hastily, a bored expression in his eyes.

'It's not that; now, please, be serious, for I want your help,' she said; 'and if I choose my words poorly you must be patient with my ignorance. The case I know will interest you, and no one else could deal with it so well. In fact, no ordinary professional man could deal with it at all, for I know of no treatment or medicine that can restore a lost sense of humour!'

'You begin to interest me with your "case,"' he replied, and made himself comfortable to listen.

Mrs Sivendson drew a sigh of contentment as she watched him go to the tube and heard him tell the servant he was not to be disturbed.

'I believe you have read my thoughts already,' she said; 'your intuitive knowledge of what goes on in other people's minds is positively uncanny.'

Her friend shook his head and smiled as he drew his chair

up to a convenient position and prepared to listen attentively to what she had to say. He closed his eyes, as he always did when he wished to absorb the real meaning of a recital that might be inadequately expressed, for by this method he found it easier to set himself in tune with the living thoughts that lay behind the broken words.

By his friends John Silence was regarded as an eccentric, because he was rich by accident, and by choice – a doctor. That a man of independent means should devote his time to doctoring, chiefly doctoring folk who could not pay, passed their comprehension entirely. The native nobility of a soul whose first desire was to help those who could not help themselves, puzzled them. After that, it irritated them, and, greatly to his own satisfaction, they left him to his own devices.

Dr Silence was a free-lance, though, among doctors, having neither consulting-room, book-keeper, nor professional manner. He took no fees, being at heart a genuine philanthropist, yet at the same time did no harm to his fellow-practitioners, because he only accepted unremunerative cases, and cases that interested him for some very special reason. He argued that the rich could pay, and the very poor could avail themselves of organised charity, but that a very large class of ill-paid, self-respecting workers, often followers of the arts, could not afford the price of a week's comforts merely to be told to travel. And it was these he desired to help: cases often requiring special and patient study – things no doctor can give for a guinea, and that no one would dream of expecting him to give.

But there was another side to his personality and practice, and one with which we are now more directly concerned; for the cases that especially appealed to him were of no ordinary kind, but rather of that intangible, elusive, and difficult nature best described as psychical afflictions; and, though he would have been the last person himself to approve of the title, it was beyond question that he was known more or less generally as the 'Psychic Doctor.'

In order to grapple with cases of this peculiar kind, he had submitted himself to a long and severe training, at once physical, mental, and spiritual. What precisely this training had been, or where undergone, no one seemed to know – for he never spoke of it, as, indeed, he betrayed no single other characteristic of the charlatan – but the fact that it had involved a total disappearance from the world for five years, and that after he returned and began his singular practice no one ever dreamed of applying to him the so easily acquired epithet of quack, spoke much for the seriousness of his strange quest and also for the genuineness of his attainments.

For the modern physical researcher he felt the calm tolerance of the 'man who knows.' There was a trace of pity in his voice – contempt he never showed – when he spoke of their methods.

'This classification of results is uninspired work at best,' he said once to me, when I had been his confidential assistant for some years. 'It leads nowhere, and after a hundred years will lead nowhere. It is playing with the wrong end of a rather dangerous toy. Far better, it would be, to examine the causes, and then the results would so easily slip into place and explain themselves. For the sources are accessible, and open to all who have the courage to lead the life that alone make practical investigation safe and possible.'

And towards the question of clairvoyance, too, his attitude was significantly sane, for he knew how extremely rare the genuine power was, and that what is commonly called clairvoyance is nothing more than a keen power of visualising.

'It connotes a slightly increased sensibility, nothing more,' he would say. 'The true clairvoyant deplores his power, recognising that it adds a new horror to life, and is in the nature of an affliction. And you will find this always to be the real test.'

Thus it was that John Silence, this singularly developed doctor, was able to select his cases with a clear knowledge of the difference between mere hysterical delusion and the kind of psychical affliction that claimed his special powers. It was never necessary for him to resort to the cheap mysteries of divination; for, as I have heard him observe, after the solution of some peculiarly intricate problem:

'Systems of divination, from geomancy down to reading by tea-leaves, are merely so many methods of obscuring the outer vision, in order that the inner vision may become open. Once the method is mastered, no system is necessary at all.'

And the words were significant of the methods of this remarkable man, the keynote of whose power lay, perhaps, more than anything else, in the knowledge, first, that thought can act at a distance, and, secondly, that thought is dynamic and can accomplish material results.

'Learn how to *think*,' he would have expressed it, 'and you have learned to tap power at its source.'

To look at – he was now past forty – he was sparely built, with speaking brown eyes in which shone the light of knowledge and self-confidence, while at the same time they made one think of that wondrous gentleness seen most often in the eyes of animals. A close beard concealed the mouth without disguising the grim determination of lips and jaw, and the face somehow conveyed an impression of transparency, almost of light, so delicately were the features refined away. On the fine forehead was that indefinable touch of peace that comes from identifying the mind with what is permanent in the soul, and letting the impermanent slip by without power to wound or distress; while, from his manner – so gentle, quiet, sympathetic – few could have guessed the strength of purpose that burned within like a great flame.

'I think I should describe it as a psychical case,' continued the Swedish lady, obviously trying to explain herself very intelligently, 'and just the kind you like. I mean a case where the cause is hidden deep down in some spiritual distress, and —'

'But the symptoms first, please, my dear Svenska,' he interrupted, with a strangely compelling seriousness of manner, 'and your deductions afterwards.'

She turned round sharply on the edge of her chair and looked him in the face, lowering her voice to prevent her emotion betraying itself too obviously.

'In my opinion there's only one symptom,' she half whispered, as though telling something disagreeable – 'fear – simply fear.'

'Physical fear?'

'I think not; though how can I say? I think it's a horror

in the psychical region. It's no ordinary delusion; the man is quite sane; but he lives in mortal terror of something —'

'I don't know what you mean by his "psychical region,"' said the doctor, with a smile; 'though I suppose you wish me to understand that his spiritual, and not his mental, processes are affected. Anyhow, try and tell me briefly and pointedly what you know about the man, his symptoms, his need for help, *my* peculiar help, that is, and all that seems vital in the case. I promise to listen devotedly.'

'I am trying,' she continued earnestly, 'but must do so in my own words and trust to your intelligence to disentangle as I go along. He is a young author, and lives in a tiny house off Putney Heath somewhere. He writes humorous stories – quite a genre of his own: Pender – you must have heard the name – Felix Pender? Oh, the man had a great gift, and married on the strength of it; his future seemed assured. I say "had," for quite suddenly his talent utterly failed him. Worse, it became transformed into its opposite. He can no longer write a line in the old way that was bringing him success —'

Dr Silence opened his eyes for a second and looked at her.

'He still writes, then? The force has not gone?' he asked briefly, and then closed his eyes again to listen.

'He works like a fury,' she went on, 'but produces nothing' – she hesitated a moment – 'nothing that he can use or sell. His earnings have practically ceased, and he makes a precarious living by book-reviewing and odd jobs – very odd, some of them. Yet, I am certain his talent has not really deserted him finally, but is merely —'

Again Mrs Sivendson hesitated for the appropriate word.

'In abeyance,' he suggested, without opening his eyes.

'Obliterated,' she went on, after a moment to weigh the word, 'merely obliterated by something else —'

'By some *one* else?'

'I wish I knew. All I can say is that he is haunted, and temporarily his sense of humour is shrouded – gone – replaced by something dreadful that writes other things. Unless something competent is done, he will simply starve to death. Yet he is afraid to go to a doctor for fear of being pronounced insane; and, anyhow, a man can hardly ask a doctor to take a guinea to restore a vanished sense of humour, can he?'

'Has he tried anyone at all —?'

'Not doctors yet. He tried some clergymen and religious people; but they *know* so little and have so little intelligent sympathy. And most of them are so busy balancing on their own little pedestals —'

John Silence stopped her tirade with a gesture.

'And how is it that you know so much about him?' he asked gently.

'I know Mrs Pender well – I knew her before she married him —'

'And is she a cause, perhaps?'

'Not in the least. She is devoted; a woman very well educated, though without being really intelligent, and with so little sense of humour herself that she always laughs at the wrong places. But she has nothing to do with the cause of his distress; and, indeed, has chiefly guessed it from observing him, rather than from what little he has told her. And he, you know, is a really lovable fellow, hard-working, patient – altogether worth saving.'

Dr Silence opened his eyes and went over to ring for tea. He did not know very much more about the case of the humorist than when he first sat down to listen; but he realised that no amount of words from his Swedish friend would help to reveal the real facts. A personal interview with the author himself could alone do that.

'All humorists are worth saving,' he said with a smile, as she poured out tea. 'We can't afford to lose a single one in these strenuous days. I will go and see your friend at the first opportunity.'

She thanked him elaborately, effusively, with many words, and he, with much difficulty, kept the conversation thenceforward strictly to the teapot.

And, as a result of this conversation, and a little more he had gathered by means best known to himself and his secretary, he was whizzing in his motor-car one afternoon a few days later up the Putney Hill to have his first interview with Felix Pender, the humorous writer who was the victim of some mysterious malady in his 'psychical region' that had obliterated his sense of the comic and threatened to wreck his life and destroy his talent. And his desire to help was probably of equal strength with his desire to know and to investigate.

The motor stopped with a deep purring sound, as though a great black panther lay concealed within its hood, and the doctor – the 'psychic doctor,' as he was sometimes called – stepped out through the gathering fog, and walked across the tiny garden that held a blackened fir tree and a stunted laurel shrubbery. The house was very small, and it was some time before anyone answered the bell. Then, suddenly, a light appeared in the hall, and he saw a pretty little woman standing on the top step begging him to come in. She was dressed in grey, and the gaslight fell on a mass of deliberately brushed light hair. Stuffed, dusty birds, and a shabby array of African spears, hung on the wall behind her. A hat-rack, with a bronze plate full of very large cards, led his eye swiftly to a dark staircase beyond. Mrs Pender had round eyes like a child's, and she greeted him with an effusiveness that barely concealed her emotion, yet strove to appear naturally cordial. Evidently she had been looking out for his arrival, and had outrun the servant girl. She was a little breathless.

'I hope you've not been kept waiting – I think it's *most* good of you to come —' she began, and then stopped sharp when she saw his face in the gaslight. There was something in Dr Silence's look that did not encourage more talk. He was in earnest now, if ever man was.

'Good evening, Mrs Pender,' he said, with a quiet smile that won confidence, yet deprecated unnecessary words, 'the fog delayed me a little. I am glad to see you.'

They went into a dingy sitting-room at the back of the house, neatly furnished but depressing. Books stood in a row upon the mantelpiece. The fire had evidently just been lit. It smoked in great puffs into the room.

'Mrs Sivendson said she thought you might be able to come,' ventured the little woman again, looking up engagingly into his face and betraying anxiety and eagerness in every gesture. 'But I hardly dared to believe it. I think it is really too good of you. My husband's case is so peculiar

24

that — well, you know, I am quite sure any *ordinary* doctor would say at once the asylum —'

'Isn't he in, then?' asked Dr Silence gently.

'In the asylum?' she gasped. 'Oh dear, no — not yet!'

'In the house, I meant,' he laughed.

She gave a great sigh.

'He'll be back any minute now,' she replied, obviously relieved to see him laugh; 'but the fact is, we didn't expect you so early — I mean, my husband hardly thought you would come at all.'

'I am always delighted to come — when I am really wanted, and can be of help,' he said quickly; 'and, perhaps, it's all for the best that your husband is out, for now that we are alone you can tell me something about his difficulties. So far, you know, I have heard very little.'

Her voice trembled as she thanked him, and when he came and took a chair close beside her she actually had difficulty in finding words with which to begin.

'In the first place,' she began timidly, and then continuing with a nervous incoherent rush of words, 'he will be simply delighted that you've really come, because he said you were the only person he would consent to see at all — the only doctor, I mean. But, of course, he doesn't know how frightened I am, or how much I have noticed. He pretends with me that it's just a nervous breakdown, and I'm sure he doesn't realise all the odd things I've noticed him doing. But the main thing, I suppose —'

'Yes, the main thing, Mrs Pender,' he said encouragingly, noticing her hesitation.

'— is that he thinks we are not alone in the house. That's the chief thing.'

'Tell me more facts — just facts.'

'It began last summer when I came back from Ireland; he had been here alone for six weeks, and I thought him looking tired and queer — ragged and scattered about the face, if you know what I mean, and his manner worn out. He said he had been writing hard, but his inspiration had somehow failed him, and he was dissatisfied with his work. His sense of humour was leaving him, or changing into something else, he said. There was something in the house,

25

he declared, that' – she emphasised the words – 'prevented his feeling funny.'

'Something in the house that prevented his feeling funny,' repeated the doctor. 'Ah, now we're getting to the heart of it!'

'Yes,' she resumed vaguely; 'that's what he kept saying.'

'And what was it he *did* that you thought strange?' he asked sympathetically. 'Be brief, or he may be here before you finish.'

'Very small things, but significant it seemed to me. He changed his workroom from the library, as we call it, to the sitting-room. He said all his characters became wrong and terrible in the library; they altered, so that he felt like writing tragedies – vile, debased tragedies, the tragedies of broken souls. But now he says the same of the sitting-room, and he's gone back to the library.'

'Ah!'

'You see, there's so little I can tell you,' she went on, with increasing speed and countless gestures. 'I mean it's only very small things he does and says that are queer. What frightens me is that he assumes there is someone else in the house all the time – someone I never see. He does not actually say so, but on the stairs I've seen him standing aside to let someone pass; I've seen him open a door to let someone in or out; and often in our bedroom he puts chairs about as though for someone else to sit in. Oh – oh, yes, and once or twice,' she cried – 'once or twice —'

She paused, and looked about her with a startled air.

'Yes?'

'Once or twice,' she resumed hurriedly, as though she heard a sound that alarmed her, 'I've heard him running – coming in and out of the rooms breathless as if something were after him —'

The door opened while she was still speaking, cutting her words off in the middle, and a man came into the room. He was dark and clean-shaven, sallow rather, with the eyes of imagination, and dark hair growing scantily about the temples. He was dressed in a shabby tweed suit, and wore an untidy flannel collar at the neck. The dominant expression of his face was startled – hunted; an expression that might any moment leap into the dreadful stare of terror and announce a total loss of self-control.

The moment he saw his visitor a smile spread over his worn features, and he advanced to shake hands.

'I hoped you would come; Mrs Sivendson said you might be able to find time,' he said simply. His voice was thin and reedy. 'I am very glad to see you, Dr Silence. It is "Doctor," is it not?'

'Well, I am entitled to the description,' laughed the other, 'but I rarely get it. You know, I do not practice as a regular thing; that is, I only take cases that specially interest me, or —'

He did not finish the sentence, for the men exchanged a glance of sympathy that rendered it unnecessary.

'I have heard of your great kindness.'

'It's my hobby,' said the other quickly, 'and my privilege.'

'I trust you will still think so when you have heard what I have to tell you,' continued the author, a little wearily. He led the way across the hall into the little smoking-room where they could talk freely and undisturbed.

In the smoking-room, the door shut and privacy about them, Pender's attitude changed somewhat and his manner became very grave. The doctor sat opposite, where he could watch his face. Already, he saw, it looked more haggard. Evidently it cost him much to refer to his trouble at all.

'What I have is, in my belief, a profound spiritual affliction,' he began quite bluntly, looking straight into the other's eyes.

'I saw that at once,' Dr Silence said.

'Yes, you saw that, of course; my atmosphere must convey that much to anyone with psychic perceptions. Besides which, I feel sure, from all I've heard, that you are really a soul-doctor, are you not, more than a healer merely of the body?'

'You think of me too highly,' returned the other; 'though I prefer cases, as you know, in which the spirit is disturbed first, the body afterwards.'

'I understand, yes. Well, I have experienced a curious disturbance in – *not* in my physical region primarily. I mean my nerves are all right, and my body is all right. I have no

27

delusions exactly, but my spirit is tortured by a calamitous fear which first came upon me in a strange manner.'

John Silence leaned forward a moment and took the speaker's hand and held it in his own for a few brief seconds, closing his eyes as he did so. He was not feeling his pulse, or doing any of the things that doctors ordinarily do; he was merely absorbing into himself the main note of the man's mental condition, so as to get completely his own point of view, and thus be able to treat his case with true sympathy. A very close observer might perhaps have noticed that a slight tremor ran through his frame after he had held the hand for a few seconds.

'Tell me quite frankly, Mr Pender,' he said soothingly releasing the hand, and with deep attention in his manner, 'tell me all the steps that led to the beginning of this invasion. I mean tell me what the particular drug was, and why you took it, and how it affected you —'

'Then you know it began with a drug!' cried the author, with undisguised astonishment.

'I only know from what I observe in you, and in its effect upon myself. You are in a surprising psychical condition. Certain portions of your atmosphere are vibrating at a far greater rate than others. This is the effect of a drug, but of no ordinary drug. Allow me to finish, please. If the higher rate of vibration spreads all over, you will become, of course, permanently cognisant of a much larger world than the one you know normally. If, on the other hand, the rapid portion sinks back to the usual rate, you will lose these occasional increased perceptions you now have.'

'You amaze me!' exclaimed the author; 'for your words exactly describe what I have been feeling —'

'I mention this only in passing, and to give you confidence before you approach the account of your real affliction,' continued the doctor. 'All perception, as you know, is the result of vibrations; and clairvoyance simply means becoming sensitive to an increased scale of vibrations. The awakening of the inner senses we hear so much about means no more than that. Your partial clairvoyance is easily explained. The only thing that puzzles me is how you managed to procure the drug, for it is not easy to get in pure form, and no adulterated tincture could have given you the terrific impetus I see you have acquired. But, please proceed now and tell me your story in your own way.'

'This *Cannabis indica*,' the author went on, 'came into my possession last autumn while my wife was away. I need not explain how I got it, for that has no importance; but it was the genuine fluid extract, and I could not resist the temptation to make an experiment. One of its effects, as you know, is to induce torrential laughter —'

'Yes; sometimes.'

'— I am a writer of humorous tales, and I wished to increase my own sense of laughter – to see the ludicrous from an abnormal point of view. I wished to study it a bit, if possible, and —'

'Tell me!'

'I took an experimental dose. I starved for six hours to hasten the effect, locked myself into this room, and gave orders not to be disturbed. Then I swallowed the stuff and waited.'

'And the effect?'

'I waited one hour, two, three, four, five hours. Nothing happened. No laughter came, but only a great weariness instead. Nothing in the room or in my thoughts came within a hundred miles of a humorous aspect.'

'Always a most uncertain drug,' interrupted the doctor. 'We make very small use of it on that account.'

'At two o'clock in the morning I felt so hungry and tired that I decided to give up the experiment and wait no longer. I drank some milk and went upstairs to bed. I felt flat and disappointed. I fell asleep at once and must have slept for about an hour, when I awoke suddenly with a great noise in my ears. It was the noise of my own laughter! I was simply shaking with merriment. At first I was bewildered and thought I had been laughing in dreams, but a moment later I remembered the drug, and was delighted to think that after all I had got an effect. It had been working all along, only I had miscalculated the time. The only unpleasant thing *then* was an odd feeling that I had not waked naturally, but had been wakened by someone else – deliberately. This came to me as a certainty in the middle of my noisy laughter and distressed me.'

'Any impression who it could have been?' asked the doctor, now listening with close attention to every word, very much on the alert.

Pender hesitated and tried to smile. He brushed his hair from his forehead with a nervous gesture.

'You must tell me all your impressions, even your fancies; they are quite as important as your certainties.'

'I have a vague idea that it was someone connected with my forgotten dream, someone who had been at me in my sleep, someone of great strength and great ability – of great force – quite an unusual personality – and, I was certain, too – a woman.'

'A good woman?' asked John Silence quietly.

Pender started a little at the question and his sallow face flushed; it seemed to surprise him. But he shook his head quickly with an indefinable look of horror.

'Evil,' he answered briefly, 'appallingly evil, and yet mingled with the sheer wickedness of it also a certain perverseness – the perversity of the unbalanced mind.'

He hesitated a moment and looked up sharply at his interlocutor. A shade of suspicion showed itself in his eyes.

'No,' laughed the doctor, 'you need not fear that I'm merely humouring you, or think you mad. Far from it. Your story interests me exceedingly and you furnish me unconsciously with a number of clues as you tell it. You see, I possess some knowledge of my own as to these psychic byways.'

'I was shaking with such violent laughter,' continued the narrator, reassured in a moment, 'though with no clear idea what was amusing me, that I had the greatest difficulty in getting up for the matches, and was afraid I should frighten the servants overhead with my explosions. When the gas was lit I found the room empty, of course, and the door locked as usual. Then I half dressed and went out on to the landing, my hilarity better under control, and proceeded to go downstairs. I wished to record my sensations. I stuffed a handkerchief into my mouth so as not to scream aloud and communicate my hysterics to the entire household.'

'And the presence of this – this —?'

'It was hanging about me all the time,' said Pender, 'but for the moment it seemed to have withdrawn. Probably, too, my laughter killed all other emotions.'

'And how long did you take getting downstairs?'

'I was just coming to that. I see you know all my "symptoms" in advance, as it were; for, of course, I thought I should never get to the bottom. Each step seemed to take five minutes, and crossing the narrow hall at the foot of the stairs – well, I could have sworn it was half an hour's journey had not my watch certified that it was a few seconds. Yet I walked fast and tried to push on. It was no good. I walked apparently without advancing, and at that rate it would have taken me a week to get down Putney Hill.'

'An experimental dose radically alters the scale of time and space sometimes —'

'But, when at last I got into my study and lit the gas, the change came horridly and sudden as a flash of lightning. It was like a douche of icy water, and in the middle of this storm of laughter —'

'Yes; what?' asked the doctor, leaning forward and peering into his eyes.

'— I was overwhelmed with terror,' said Pender, lowering his reedy voice at the mere recollection of it.

He paused a moment and mopped his forehead. The scared, hunted look in his eyes now dominated the whole face. Yet, all the time, the corners of his mouth hinted of possible laughter as though the recollection of that merriment still amused him. The combination of fear and laughter in his face was very curious, and lent great conviction to his story; it also lent a bizarre expression of horror to his gestures.

'Terror, was it?' repeated the doctor soothingly.

'Yes, terror; for, though the Thing that woke me seemed to have gone, the memory of it still frightened me, and I collapsed into a chair. Then I locked the door and tried to reason with myself, but the drug made my movements so prolonged that it took me five minutes to reach the door, and another five to get back to the chair again. The laughter, too, kept bubbling up inside me – great wholesome laughter that shook me like gusts of wind – so that even my terror almost made me laugh. Oh, but I may tell you, Dr Silence, it was altogether vile, that mixture of fear and laughter, altogether vile!

'Then, all at once, the things in the room again presented their funny side to me and set me off laughing more furiously than ever. The bookcase was ludicrous, the armchair a perfect clown, the way the clock looked at me on the mantelpiece too comic for words; the arrangement of papers and inkstand on the desk tickled me till I roared and shook and held my sides and the tears streamed down my cheeks. And that footstool! Oh, that absurd footstool!'

He lay back in his chair, laughing to himself and holding up his hands at the thought of it, and at the sight of him Dr Silence laughed too.

'Go on, please,' he said, 'I quite understand. I know something myself of the hashish laughter.'

The author pulled himself together and resumed, his face growing quickly grave again.

'So, you see, side by side with this extravagant, apparently causeless merriment, there was also an extravagant, apparently causeless terror. The drug produced the laughter, I knew; but what brought in the terror I could not imagine. Everywhere behind the fun lay the fear. It was terror masked by cap and bells; and I became the playground for two opposing emotions, armed and fighting to the death. Gradually, then, the impression grew in me that this fear was caused by the invasion – so you called it just now – of the "person" who had wakened me: she was utterly evil; inimical to my soul, or at least to all in me that wished for good. There I stood, sweating and trembling, laughing at everything in the room, yet all the while with this white terror mastering my heart. And this creature was putting – putting her —'

He hesitated again, using his handkerchief freely.

'Putting what?'

'— putting ideas into my mind,' he went on, glancing nervously about the room. 'Actually tapping my thought-stream so as to switch off the usual current and inject her own. How mad that sounds! I know it, but it's true. It's the only way I can express it. Moreover, while the operation terrified me, the skill with which it was accomplished filled me afresh with laughter at the clumsiness of men by comparison. Our ignorant, bungling methods of teaching the minds of others, of inculcating ideas, and so on, overwhelmed me with laughter when I understood this superior and diabolical method. Yet my laughter seemed hollow and ghastly, and ideas of evil and tragedy trod close upon the heels of the comic. Oh, doctor, I tell you again, it was unnerving!'

John Silence sat with his head thrust forward to catch every word of the story which the other continued to pour out in nervous, jerky sentences and lowered voice.

'You saw nothing – no one – all this time?' he asked.

'Not with my eyes. There was no visual hallucination. But in my mind there began to grow the vivid picture of a woman – large, dark-skinned, with white teeth and masculine features, and one eye – the left – so drooping as to appear almost closed. Oh, such a face —!'

'A face you would recognise again?'

Pender laughed dreadfully.

'I wish I could forget it,' he whispered, 'I only wish I could forget it!' Then he sat forward in his chair suddenly, and grasped the doctor's hand with an emotional gesture.

'I *must* tell you how grateful I am for your patience and sympathy,' he cried, with a tremor in his voice, 'and – that you do not think me mad. I have told no one else a quarter of this, and the mere freedom of speech – the relief of sharing my affliction with another – has helped me already more than I can possibly say.'

Dr Silence pressed his hand and looked steadily into the frightened eyes. His voice was very gentle when he replied.

'Your case, you know, is very singular, but of absorbing interest to me,' he said, 'for it threatens, not your physical existence, but the temple of your psychical existence – the inner life. Your mind would not be permanently affected here and now, in this world; but in the existence after the body is left behind, you might wake up with your spirit so twisted, so distorted, so befouled, that you would be *spiritually insane* – a far more radical condition than merely being insane here.'

There came a strange hush over the room, and between the two men sitting there facing one another.

'Do you really mean – Good Lord!' stammered the author as soon as he could find his tongue.

'What I mean in detail will keep till a little later, and I need only say now that I should not have spoken in this way unless I were quite positive of being able to help you. Oh, there's no doubt as to that, believe me. In the first place, I am very familiar with the workings of this extraordinary drug, this drug which has had the chance effect of opening you up to the forces of another region; and, in the second, I have a firm belief in the reality of super-sensuous occurrences as well as considerable knowledge of psychic processes acquired by long and painful experiment. The rest is, or should be, merely sympathetic treatment and practical application. The hashish has partially opened another world to you by increasing your rate of psychical vibration, and thus rendering you abnormally sensitive. Ancient forces attached to this house have attacked you. For the moment I am only puzzled as to their precise nature; for were they of an ordinary character, I should myself be psychic enough to feel them. Yet I am conscious of feeling nothing as yet. But now, please continue, Mr Pender, and tell me the rest of your wonderful story; and when you have finished, I will talk about the means of cure.'

Pender shifted his chair a little closer to the friendly doctor and then went on in the same nervous voice with his narrative.

'After making some notes of my impressions I finally got upstairs again to bed. It was four o'clock in the morning. I laughed all the way up – at the grotesque banisters, the droll physiognomy of the staircase window, the burlesque grouping of the furniture, and the memory of that outrageous footstool in the room below; but nothing more happened to alarm or disturb me, and I woke late in the morning after a dreamless sleep, none the worse for my experiment except for a slight headache and a coldness of the extremities due to lowered circulation.'

'Fear gone, too?' asked the doctor.

'I seemed to have forgotten it, or at least ascribed it to

mere nervousness. Its reality had gone, anyhow for the time, and all that day I wrote and wrote and wrote. My sense of laughter seemed wonderfully quickened and my characters acted without effort out of the heart of true humour. I was exceedingly pleased with this result of my experiment. But when the stenographer had taken her departure and I came to read over the pages she had typed out, I recalled her sudden glances of surprise and the odd way she had looked up at me while I was dictating. I was amazed at what I read and could hardly believe I had uttered it.'

'And why?'

'It was so distorted. The words, indeed, were mine so far as I could remember, but the meanings seemed strange. It frightened me. The sense was so altered. At the very places where my characters were intended to tickle the ribs, only curious emotions of sinister amusement resulted. Dreadful innuendoes had managed to creep into the phrases. There was laughter of a kind, but it was bizarre, horrible, distressing; and my attempt at analysis only increased my dismay. The story, as it read then, made me shudder, for by virtue of these slight changes it had come somehow to hold the soul of horror, of horror disguised as merriment. The framework of humour was there, if you understand me, but the characters had turned sinister, and their laughter was evil.'

'Can you show me this writing?'

The author shook his head.

'I destroyed it,' he whispered. 'But, in the end, though of course much perturbed about it, I persuaded myself that it was due to some after-effect of the drug, a sort of reaction that gave a twist to my mind and made me read macabre interpretations into words and situations that did not properly hold them.'

'And, meanwhile, did the presence of this person leave you?'

'No; that stayed more or less. When my mind was actively employed I forgot it, but when idle, dreaming, or doing nothing in particular, there she was beside me, influencing my mind horribly —'

'In what way, precisely?' interrupted the doctor.

'Evil, scheming thoughts came to me, visions of crime, hateful pictures of wickedness, and the kind of bad imagination that so far has been foreign, indeed impossible, to my normal nature —'

'The pressure of the Dark Powers upon the personality,' murmured the doctor, making a quick note.

'Eh? I didn't quite catch —'

'Pray go on. I am merely making notes; you shall know their purport fully later.'

'Even when my wife returned I was still aware of this Presence in the house; it associated itself with my inner personality in most intimate fashion; and outwardly I always felt oddly constrained to be polite and respectful towards it – to open doors, provide chairs and hold myself carefully deferential when it was about. It became very compelling at last, and, if I failed in any little particular, I seemed to know that it pursued me about the house, from one room to another, haunting my very soul in its inmost abode. It certainly came before my wife so far as my attentions were concerned.

'But let me first finish the story of my experimental dose, for I took it again the third night, and underwent a very similar experience, delayed like the first in coming, and then carrying me off my feet when it did come with a rush of this false demon-laughter. This time, however, there was a reversal of the changed scale of space and time; it shortened, instead of lengthened, so that I dressed and got downstairs in about twenty seconds, and the couple of hours I stayed and worked in the study passed literally like a period of ten minutes.'

'That is often true of an overdose,' interjected the doctor, 'and you may go a mile in a few minutes, or a few yards in a quarter of an hour. It is quite incomprehensible to those who never experienced it, and is a curious proof that time and space are merely forms of thought.'

'This time,' Pender went on, talking more and more rapidly in his excitement, 'another extraordinary effect came to me, and I experienced a curious changing of the senses, so that I perceived external things through one large main sense-channel instead of through the five divisions known as sight, smell, touch, and so forth. You will, I know, understand me when I tell you that I *heard* sights and *saw* sounds. No language can make this comprehensible, of course, and I can only say, for instance, that the striking of the clock I saw as a visible picture in the air before me. I saw the sounds of the tinkling bell. And in precisely the same way I heard the colours in the room, especially the colours of those books in the shelf behind you. The red bindings I heard in deep sounds, and the yellow covers of the French bindings next to them made a shrill, piercing note not unlike the chattering of starlings. That brown bookcase muttered, and those green curtains opposite kept up a constant sort of rippling sound like the lower notes of a wood-horn. But I only was conscious of these sounds when I looked steadily at the different objects, and thought about them. The room, you understand, was not full of a chorus of notes; but when I concentrated my mind upon a colour, I heard, as well as saw, it.'

'That is a known, though rarely-obtained, effect of *Cannabis indica*,' observed the doctor. 'And it provoked laughter again, did it?'

'Only the muttering of the cupboard bookcase made me laugh. It was so like a great animal trying to get itself noticed, and made me think of a performing bear – which is full of a kind of pathetic humour, you know. But this mingling of the senses produced no confusion in my brain. On the contrary, I was unusually clear-headed and experienced an intensification of consciousness, and felt marvellously alive and keen-minded.

'Moreover, when I took up a pencil in obedience to an impulse to sketch – a talent not normally mine – I found that I could draw nothing but heads, nothing, in fact, but one head – always the same – the head of a dark-skinned woman, with huge and terrible features and a very drooping left eye; and so well drawn, too, that I was amazed, as you may imagine —'

'And the expression of the face —?'

Pender hesitated a moment for words, casting about with his hands in the air and hunching his shoulders. A perceptible shudder ran over him.

'What I can only describe as – *blackness*,' he replied in a low tone; 'the face of a dark and evil sound.'

'You destroyed that, too?' queried the doctor sharply.

'No; I have kept the drawings,' he said, with a laugh, and rose to get them from a drawer in the writing-desk behind him.

'Here is all that remains of the pictures, you see,' he added, pushing a number of loose sheets under the doctor's eyes; 'nothing but a few scrawly lines. That's all I found the next morning. I had really drawn no heads at all – nothing but those lines and blots and wriggles. The pictures were entirely subjective, and existed only in my mind which constructed them out of a few wild strokes of the pen. Like the altered scale of space and time it was a complete delusion. These all passed, of course, with the passing of the drug's effects. But the other thing did not pass. I mean, the presence of that Dark Soul remained with me. It is here still. It is real. I don't know how I can escape from it.'

'It is attached to the house, not to you personally. You must leave the house.'

'Yes. Only I cannot afford to leave the house, for my work is my sole means of support, and – well, you see, since this change I cannot even write. They are horrible, these mirthless tales I now write, with their mockery of laughter, their diabolical suggestion. Horrible! I shall go mad if this continues.'

He screwed his face up and looked about the room as though he expected to see some haunting shape.

'The influence in this house, induced by my experiment, has killed in a flash, in a sudden stroke, the sources of my humour, and, though I still go on writing funny tales – I have a certain name, you know – my inspiration has dried up, and much of what I write I have to burn – yes, doctor, to burn, before anyone sees it.'

'As utterly alien to your own mind and personality?'

'Utterly! As though someone else had written it —'

'Ah!'

'And shocking!' He passed his hand over his eyes a moment and let the breath escape softly through his teeth. 'Yet most damnably clever in the consummate way the vile suggestions are insinuated under cover of a kind of high drollery. My stenographer left me, of course – and I've been afraid to take another –'

John Silence got up and began to walk about the room leisurely without speaking; he appeared to be examining the pictures on the wall and reading the names of the books lying about. Presently he paused on the hearthrug, with his back to the fire, and turned to look his patient quietly in the eyes. Pender's face was grey and drawn; the hunted expression dominated it; the long recital had told upon him.

'Thank you, Mr Pender,' he said, a curious glow showing about his fine, quiet face, 'thank you for the sincerity and frankness of your account. But I think now there is nothing further I need ask you.' He indulged in a long scrutiny of the author's haggard features, drawing purposely the man's eyes to his own and then meeting them with a look of power and confidence calculated to inspire even the feeblest soul with courage. 'And, to begin with,' he added, smiling pleasantly, 'let me assure you without delay that you need have no alarm, for you are no more insane or deluded than I myself am –'

Pender heaved a deep sigh and tried to return the smile.

'– and this is simply a case, so far as I can judge at present, of a very singular psychical invasion, and a very sinister one, too, if you perhaps understand what I mean –'

'It's an odd expression; you used it before, you know,' said the author wearily, yet eagerly listening to every word of the diagnosis, and deeply touched by the intelligent sympathy which did not at once indicate the lunatic asylum.

'Possibly,' returned the other, 'and an odd affliction too, you'll allow, yet one not unknown to the nations of antiquity, not to those moderns, perhaps, who recognise the freedom of action under certain pathogenic conditions between this world and another.'

'And you think,' asked Pender hastily, 'that it is all primarily due to the *Cannabis*? There is nothing radically amiss with myself – nothing incurable, or –?'

'Due entirely to the overdose,' Dr Silence replied emphatically, 'to the drug's direct action upon your psychical being. It rendered you ultra-sensitive and made you respond to an increased rate of vibration. And, let me tell you, Mr

Pender, that your experiment might have had results far more dire. It has brought you into touch with a somewhat singular class of Invisible, but of one, I think, chiefly human in character. You might, however, just as easily have been drawn out of human range altogether, and the results of such a contingency would have been exceedingly terrible. Indeed, you would not now be here to tell the tale. I need not alarm you on that score, but mention it as a warning you will not misunderstand or underrate after what you have been through.

'You look puzzled. You do not quite gather what I am driving at; and it is not to be expected that you should, for you, I suppose, are the nominal Christian with the nominal Christian's lofty standard of ethics, and his utter ignorance of spiritual possibilities. Beyond a somewhat childish understanding of "spiritual wickedness in high places", you probably have no conception of what is possible once you break down the slender gulf that is mercifully fixed between you and that Outer World. But my studies and training have taken me far outside these orthodox trips, and I have made experiments that I could scarcely speak to you about in language that would be intelligible to you.'

He paused a moment to note the breathless interest of Pender's face and manner. Every word he uttered was calculated; he knew exactly the value and effect of the emotions he desired to waken in the heart of the afflicted being before him.

'And from certain knowledge I have gained through various experiences,' he continued calmly, 'I can diagnose your case, as I said before, to be one of psychical invasion.'

'And the nature of this – er – invasion?' stammered the bewildered writer of humorous tales.

'There is no reason why I should not say at once that I do not yet quite know,' replied Dr Silence. 'I may first have to make one or two experiments —'

'On me?' gasped Pender, catching his breath.

'Not exactly,' the doctor said, with a grave smile, 'but with your assistance, perhaps. I shall want to test the conditions of the house – to ascertain, if possible, the character of the forces, of this strange personality that has been haunting you —'

'At present you have no idea exactly who – what – why—?' asked the other in a wild flurry of interest, dread and amazement.

'I have a very good idea, but no proof rather,' returned the doctor. 'The effects of the drug in altering the scale of time and space, and merging the senses have nothing primarily to do with the invasion. They come to anyone who is fool enough to take an experimental dose. It is the other features of your case that are unusual. You see, you are now in touch with certain violent emotions, desires, purposes, still active in this house, that were produced in the past by some powerful and evil personality that lived here. How long ago, or why they still persist so forcibly, I cannot positively say. But I should judge that they are merely forces acting automatically with the momentum of their terrific original impetus.'

'Not directed by a living being, a conscious will, you mean?'

'Possibly not – but none the less dangerous on that account, and more difficult to deal with. I cannot explain to you in a few minutes the nature of such things, for you have not made the studies that would enable you to follow me; but I have reason to believe that on the dissolution at death of a human being, its forces may still persist and continue to act in a blind, unconscious fashion. As a rule they speedily dissipate themselves, but in the case of a very powerful personality they may last a long time. And, in some cases – of which I incline to think this is one – these forces may coalesce with certain non-human entities who thus continue their life indefinitely and increase their strength to an unbelievable degree. If the original personality was evil, the beings attracted to the left-over forces will also be evil. In this case, I think there has been an unusual and dreadful aggrandisement of the thoughts and purposes left behind long ago by a woman of consummate wickedness and great personal power of character and intellect. Now, do you begin to see what I am driving at a little?'

Pender stared fixedly at his companion, plain horror showing in his eyes. But he found nothing to say, and the doctor continued:

'In your case, predisposed by the action of the drug, you have experienced the rush of these forces in undiluted strength. They wholly obliterate in you the sense of humour, fancy, imagination – all that makes for cheerfulness and hope. They seek, though perhaps automatically only, to oust your own thoughts and establish themselves in their place. You are the victim of a psychical invasion. At the same time, you have become clairvoyant in the true sense. You are also a clairvoyant victim.'

Pender mopped his face and sighed. He left his chair and went over to the fireplace to warm himself.

'You must think me a quack to talk like this, or a madman,' laughed Dr Silence. 'But never mind that. I have come to help you, and I can help you if you will do what I tell you. It is very simple; you must leave this house at once Oh, never mind the difficulties; we will deal with those together. I can place another house at your disposal, or I would take the lease here off your hands, and later have it pulled down. Your case interests me greatly, and I mean to see you through, so that you have no anxiety, and can drop back into your old groove of work tomorrow! The drug has provided you, and therefore me, with a short-cut to a very interesting experience. I am grateful to you.'

The author poked the fire vigorously, emotion rising in him like a tide. He glanced towards the door nervously.

'There is no need to alarm your wife or to tell her the details of our conversation,' pursued the other quietly. 'Let her know that you will soon be in possession again of your sense of humour and your health, and explain that I am lending you another house for six months. Meanwhile I may have the right to use this house for a night or two for my experiment. Is that understood between us?'

'I can only thank you from the bottom of my heart,' stammered Pender, unable to find words to express his gratitude.

Then he hesitated for a moment, searching the doctor's face anxiously.

'And your experiment with the house?' he said at length.

'Of the simplest character, my dear Mr Pender. Although

I am myself an artificially trained psychic, and consequently aware of the presence of discarnate entities as a rule, I have so far felt nothing here at all. This makes me sure that the forces acting here are of an unusual description. What I propose to do is to make an experiment with a view of drawing out this evil, coaxing it from its lair, so to speak, in order that it may *exhaust itself through me* and become dissipated for ever. I have already been inoculated,' he added; 'I consider myself to be immune.'

'Heavens above!' gasped the author, collapsing on to a chair.

'Hell beneath! might be a more appropriate exclamation,' the doctor laughed. 'But seriously, Mr Pender, that is what I propose to do – with your permission.'

'Of course, of course,' cried the other, 'you may have my permission and my best wishes for success. I can see no possible objection, but —'

'But what?'

'I pray to Heaven you will not undertake this experiment alone, will you?'

'Oh, dear, no; not alone.'

'You will take a companion with good nerves, and reliable in case of disaster, won't you?'

'I shall bring two companions,' the doctor said.

'Ah, that's better. I feel easier. I am sure you must have among your acquaintances men who —'

'I shall not think of bringing men, Mr Pender.'

The other looked up sharply.

'No, or women either; or children.'

'I don't understand. Who will you bring, then?'

'Animals,' explained the doctor, unable to prevent a smile at his companion's expression of surprise – 'two animals, a cat and a dog.'

Pender stared as if his eyes would drop out upon the floor, and then led the way without another word into the adjoining room where his wife was awaiting them for tea.

2

A FEW DAYS later the humorist and his wife, with minds greatly relieved, moved into a small furnished house placed at their free disposal in another part of London; and John Silence, intent upon his approaching experiment, made ready to spend a night in the empty house on the top of Putney Hill. Only two rooms were prepared for occupation: the study on the ground floor and the bedroom immediately above it; all other doors were to be locked, and no servant was to be left in the house. The motor had orders to call for him at nine o'clock the following morning.

And, meanwhile, his secretary had instructions to look up the past history and associations of the place, and learn everything he could concerning the character of former occupants, recent or remote.

The animals, by whose sensitiveness he intended to test any unusual conditions in the atmosphere of the building, Dr Silence selected with care and judgement. He believed (and had already made curious experiments to prove it) that animals were more often, and more truly, clairvoyant than human beings. Many of them, he felt convinced, possessed powers of perception far superior to that mere keenness of the senses common to all dwellers in the wilds where the senses grow specially alert; they had what he termed 'animal clairvoyance', and from his experiments with horses, dogs, cats, and even birds, he had drawn certain deductions, which, however, need not be referred to in detail here.

Cats, in particular, he believed, were almost continuously conscious of a larger field of vision, too detailed even for a photographic camera, and quite beyond the reach of normal human organs. He had, further, observed that while dogs were usually terrified in the presence of such phenomena, cats on the other hand were soothed and satisfied. They welcomed manifestations as something belonging peculiarly to their own region.

He selected his animals, therefore, with wisdom, so that they might afford a differing test, each in its own way, and that one should not merely communicate its own excitement to the other. He took a dog and a cat.

The cat he chose, now full grown, had lived with him since kittenhood, a kittenhood of perplexing sweetness and audacious mischief. Wayward it was and fanciful, ever playing its own mysterious games in the corners of the room, jumping at invisible nothings, leaping sideways into the air and falling with tiny mocassined feet on to another part of the carpet, yet with an air of dignified earnestness which showed that the performance was necessary to its own well-being, and not done merely to impress a stupid human audience. In the middle of elaborate washing it would look up, startled, as though to stare at the approach of some Invisible, cocking its little head sideways and putting out a velvet pad to inspect cautiously. Then it would get absent-minded, and stare with equal intentness in another direction (just to confuse the onlookers), and suddenly go on furiously washing its body again, but in quite a new place. Except for a white patch on its breast it was coal black. And its name was – Smoke.

'Smoke' described its temperament as well as its appearance. Its movements, its individuality, its posing as a little furry mass of concealed mysteries, its elfin-like elusiveness, all combined to justify its name; and a subtle painter might have pictured it as a wisp of floating smoke, the fire below betraying itself at two points only – the glowing eyes.

All its forces ran to intelligence – secret intelligence, the wordless, incalculable intuition of the Cat. It was, indeed, *the* cat for the business in hand.

The selection of the dog was not so simple, for the doctor owned many; but after much deliberation he chose a collie, called Flame from his yellow coat. True, it was a trifle old, and stiff in the joints, and even beginning to grow deaf, but, on the other hand, it was a very particular friend of Smoke's and had fathered it from kittenhood upwards so that a subtle understanding existed between them. It was this that turned the balance in its favour, this and its courage. More-over, though good-tempered, it was a terrible fighter, and its anger when provoked by a righteous cause was a fury of fire, and irresistible.

It had come to him quite young, straight from the shepherd, with the air of the hills yet in its nostrils, and was then little more than skin and bones and teeth. For a collie it was sturdily built, its nose blunter than most, its yellow hair stiff rather than silky, and it had full eyes, unlike the slit eyes of its breed. Only its master could touch it, for it ignored strangers, and despised their pattings – when they dared to pat it. There was something patriarchal about the old beast. He was in earnest, and went through life with tremendous energy and big things in view, as though he had the reputation of his whole race to uphold. And to watch him fighting against odds was to understand why he was terrible.

In his relations with Smoke he was always absurdly gentle; also he was fatherly; and at the same time betrayed a certain diffidence or shyness. He recognised that Smoke called for strong yet respectful management. The cat's circuitous methods puzzled him, and his elaborate pretences perhaps shocked the dog's liking for direct, undisguised action. Yet, while he failed to comprehend these tortuous feline mysteries, he was never contemptuous or condescending; and he presided over the safety of his furry black friend somewhat as a father, loving but intuitive, might super-intend the vagaries of a wayward and talented child. And, in return, Smoke rewarded him with exhibitions of fascinating and audacious mischief.

And these brief descriptions of their characters are neces-sary for the proper understanding of what subsequently took place.

With Smoke sleeping in the folds of his fur coat, and the collie lying watchful on the seat opposite, John Silence went down in his motor after dinner on the night of November 15th.

And the fog was so dense that they were obliged to travel at quarter speed the entire way.

*   *   *

It was after ten o'clock when he dismissed the motor and entered the dingy little house with the latchkey provided by Pender. He found the hall gas turned low, and a fire in the study. Books and food had also been placed ready by the servant according to instructions. Coils of fog rushed in after him through the opened door and filled the hall and passage with its cold discomfort.

The first thing Dr Silence did was to lock up Smoke in the study with a saucer of milk before the fire, and then make a search of the house with Flame. The dog ran cheerfully behind him all the way while he tried the doors of the other rooms to make sure they were locked. He nosed about into corners and made little excursions on his own account. His manner was expectant. He knew there must be something unusual about the proceeding, because it was contrary to the habits of his whole life not to be asleep at this hour on the mat in front of the fire. He kept looking up into his master's face, as door after door was tried, with an expression of intelligent sympathy, but at the same time a certain air of disapproval. Yet everything his master did was good in his eyes, and he betrayed as little impatience as possible with all this unnecessary journeying to and fro. If the doctor was pleased to play this sort of game at such an hour of the night, it was surely not for him to object. So he played it, too; and was very busy and earnest about it into the bargain.

After an eventful search they came down again to the study, and here Dr Silence discovered Smoke washing his face calmly in front of the fire. The saucer of milk was licked dry and clean; the preliminary examination that cats always make in new surroundings had evidently been satisfactorily concluded. He drew an arm-chair up to the fire, stirred the coals into a blaze, arranged the table and lamp to his satisfaction for reading, and then prepared surreptitiously to watch the animals. He wished to observe them carefully without their being aware of it.

Now, in spite of their respective ages, it was the regular custom of these two to play together every night before sleep. Smoke always made the advances, beginning with grave impudence to pat the dog's tail, and Flame played cumbrously, with condescension. It was his duty, rather than pleasure; he was glad when it was over, and sometimes he was very determined and refused to play at all.

And this night was one of the occasions on which he was firm.

The doctor, looking cautiously over the top of his book, watched the cat begin the performance. It started by gazing with an innocent expression at the dog where he lay with nose on paws and eyes wide open in the middle of the floor.

47

Then it got up and made as though it meant to walk to the door, going deliberately and very softly. Flame's eyes followed it until it was beyond the range of sight, and then the cat turned sharply and began patting his tail tentatively with one paw. The tail moved slightly in reply, and Smoke changed paws and tapped it again. The dog, however, did not rise to play as was his wont, and the cat fell to patting it briskly with both paws. Flame still lay motionless.

This puzzled and bored the cat, and it went round and stared into its friend's face to see what was the matter. Perhaps some inarticulate message flashed from the dog's eyes into its own little brain, making it understand that the programme for the night had better not begin with play. Perhaps it only realised that its friend was immovable. But, whatever the reason, its usual persistence thenceforward deserted it, and it made no further attempts at persuasion. Smoke yielded at once to the dog's mood; it sat down where it was and began to wash.

But the washing, the doctor noted, was by no means its real purpose; it only used it to mask something else; it stopped at the most busy and furious moments and began to stare about the room. Its thoughts wandered absurdly. It peered intently at the curtains; at the shadowy corners; at empty space above; leaving its body in curiously awkward positions for whole minutes together. Then it turned sharply and stared with a sudden signal of intelligence at the dog, and Flame at once rose somewhat stiffly to his feet and began to wander aimlessly and restlessly to and fro about the floor. Smoke followed him, padding quietly at his heels. Between them they made what seemed to be a deliberate search of the room.

And, here, as he watched them, noting carefully every detail of the performance over the top of his book, yet making no effort to interfere, it seemed to the doctor that the first beginnings of a faint distress betrayed themselves in the collie, and in the cat the stirrings of a vague excitement.

He observed them closely. The fog was thick in the air, and the tobacco smoke from his pipe added to its density; the furniture at the far end stood mistily, and where the shadows congregated in hanging clouds under the ceiling, it was difficult to see clearly at all; the lamp-light only reached to a level of five feet from the floor, above which came layers of comparative darkness, so that the room appeared twice as lofty as it actually was. By means of the lamp and the fire, however, the carpet was everywhere clearly visible.

The animals made their silent tour of the floor, sometimes the dog leading, sometimes the cat; occasionally they looked at one another as though exchanging signals; and once or twice, in spite of the limited space, he lost sight of one or other among the fog and the shadows. Their curiosity, it appeared to him, was something more than the excitement lurking in the unknown territory of a strange room; yet, so far, it was impossible to test this, and he purposely kept his mind quietly receptive lest the smallest mental excitement on his part should communicate itself to the animals and thus destroy the value of their independent behaviour.

They made a very thorough journey, leaving no piece of furniture unexamined, or unsmelt. Flame led the way, walking slowly with lowered head, and Smoke followed demurely at his heels, making a transparent pretence of not being interested, yet missing nothing. And, at length, they returned, the old collie first, and came to rest on the mat before the fire. Flame rested his muzzle on his master's knee, smiling beatifically while he patted the yellow head and spoke his name; and Smoke, coming a little later, pretending he came by chance, looked from the empty saucer to his face, lapped up the milk when it was given him to the last drop, and then sprang upon his knees and curled round for the sleep it had fully earned and intended to enjoy.

Silence descended upon the room. Only the breathing of the dog upon the mat came through the deep stillness, like the pulse of time marking the minutes; and the steady drip, drip of the fog outside upon the window-ledges dismally testified to the inclemency of the night beyond. And the soft crashings of the coals as the fire settled down into the grate became less and less audible as the fire sank and the flames resigned their fierceness.

It was now well after eleven o'clock, and Dr Silence devoted himself again to his book. He read the words on the printed page and took in their meaning superficially, yet without starting into life the correlations of thought and suggestion that should accompany interesting reading. Underneath, all the while his mental energies were absorbed in watching, listening, waiting for what might come. He was not over sanguine himself, yet he did not wish to be taken by surprise. Moreover, the animals, his sensitive barometers, had incontinently gone to sleep.

After reading a dozen pages, however, he realised that his mind was really occupied in reviewing the features of Pender's extraordinary story, and that it was no longer necessary to steady his imagination by studying the dull paragraphs detailed in the pages before him. He laid down his book accordingly, and allowed his thoughts to dwell upon the features of the case. Speculations as to the meaning, however, he rigorously suppressed, knowing that such thoughts would act upon his imagination like wind upon the glowing embers of a fire.

As the night wore on the silence grew deeper and deeper, and only at rare intervals he heard the sound of wheels on the main road a hundred yards away, where the horses went at a walking pace owing to the density of the fog. The echo of pedestrian footsteps no longer reached him, the clamour of occasional voices no longer came down the side street. The night, muffled by fog, shrouded by veils of ultimate mystery, hung about the haunted villa like a doom. Nothing in the house stirred. Stillness, in a thick blanket, lay over the upper storeys. Only the mist in the room grew more dense, he thought, and the damp cold more penetrating. Certainly, from time to time, he shivered.

The collie, now deep in slumber, moved occasionally – grunted, sighed, or twitched his legs in dreams. Smoke lay on his knees, a pool of warm, black fur, only the closest observation detecting the movement of his sleek sides. It was difficult to distinguish exactly where his head and body joined in that circle of glistening hair; only a black satin nose and a tiny tip of pink tongue betrayed the secret.

Dr Silence watched him, and felt comfortable. The collie's breathing was soothing. The fire was well built, and would burn for another two hours without attention. He was not conscious of the least nervousness. He particularly wished to remain in his ordinary and normal state of mind, and to force nothing. If sleep came naturally, he would let it come – and even welcome it. The coldness of the room, when the fire died down later, would be sure to wake him again; and it would then be time enough to carry these sleeping barometers up to bed. From various psychic premonitions he knew quite well that the night would not pass without adventure; but he did not wish to force its arrival; and he wished to remain normal, and let the animals remain normal, so that, when it came, it would be unattended by excitement or by any straining of the attention. Many experiments had made him wise. And, for the rest, he had no fear.

Accordingly, after a time, he did fall asleep as he had expected, and the last thing he remembered, before oblivion slipped up over his eyes like soft wool, was the picture of Flame stretching all four legs at once, and sighing noisily as he sought a more comfortable position for his paws and muzzle upon the mat.

* * *

It was a good deal later when he became aware that a weight lay upon his chest, and that something was pencilling over his face and mouth. A soft touch on the cheek woke him. Something was patting him.

He sat up with a jerk, and found himself staring straight into a pair of brilliant eyes, half green, half black. Smoke's face lay level with his own; and the cat had climbed up with its front paws upon his chest.

The lamp had burned low and the fire was nearly out, yet Dr Silence saw in a moment that the cat was in an excited state. It kneaded with its front paws into his chest, shifting from one to the other. He felt them prodding against him. It lifted a leg very carefully and patted his cheek gingerly. Its fur, he saw, was standing ridgewise upon its back; the ears were flattened back somewhat; the tail was switching sharply. The cat, of course, had wakened him with a purpose, and the instant he realised this, he set it upon the arm of the chair and sprang up with a quick turn to face the empty room behind him. By some curious instinct, his arms of their own accord assumed an attitude of defence in front of him, as though to ward off something that threatened his safety. Yet nothing was visible. Only shapes of fog hung about rather heavily in the air, moving slightly to and fro.

His mind was now fully alert, and the last vestiges of sleep gone. He turned the lamp higher and peered about him. Two things he became aware of at once: one, that Smoke, while excited, was *pleasurably* excited; the other, that the collie was no longer visible upon the mat at his feet. He had crept away to the corner of the wall farthest from the window, and lay watching the room with wideopen eyes, in which lurked plainly something of alarm.

Something in the dog's behaviour instantly struck Dr Silence as unusual, and, calling him by name, he moved across to pat him. Flame got up, wagged his tail, and came over slowly to the rug, uttering a low sound that was half growl, half whine. He was evidently perturbed about something, and his master was proceeding to administer comfort when his attention was suddenly drawn to the antics of his other four-footed companion, the cat.

And what he saw filled him with something like amazement.

Smoke had jumped down from the back of the arm-chair and now occupied the middle of the carpet, where, with tail erect and legs stiff as ramrods, it was steadily pacing backwards and forwards in a narrow space, uttering as it did so, those curious little gutteral sounds of pleasure that only an animal of the feline species knows how to make expressive of supreme happiness. Its stiffened legs and arched back made it appear larger than usual, and the black visage wore a smile of beautific joy. Its eyes blazed magnificently; it was in an ecstasy.

At the end of every few paces it turned sharply and stalked back again along the same line, padding softly, and purring like a roll of little muffled drums. It behaved precisely as though it were rubbing against the ankles of someone who remained invisible. A thrill ran down the doctor's spine as he stood and stared. His experiment was growing interesting at last.

He called the collie's attention to his friend's performance to see whether he too was aware of anything standing there upon the carpet, and the dog's behaviour was significant and corroborative. He came as far as his master's knees and then stopped dead, refusing to investigate closely. In vain Dr Silence urged him; he wagged his tail, whined a little, and stood in a half-crouching attitude, staring alternately at the cat and at his master's face. He was, apparently, both puzzled and alarmed, and the whine went deeper and deeper down into his throat till it changed into an ugly snarl of awakening anger.

Then the doctor called to him in a tone of command he had never known to be disregarded; but still the dog, though springing up in response, declined to move nearer. He made tentative motions, pranced a little like a dog about to take to water, pretended to bark, and ran to and fro on the carpet. So far there was no actual fear in his manner, but he was uneasy and anxious, and nothing would induce him to go within touching distance of the walking cat. Once he made a complete circuit, but always carefully out of reach; and in the end he returned to his master's legs and rubbed vigorously against him. Flame did not like the performance at all: that much was quite clear.

For several minutes John Silence watched the performance of the cat with profound attention and without interfering. Then he called to the animal by name.

'Smoke, you mysterious beastie, what in the world are you about?' he said, in a coaxing tone.

The cat looked up at him for a moment, smiling in its ecstasy, blinking its eyes, but too happy to pause. He spoke to it again. He called to it several times, and each time it turned upon him its blazing eyes, drunk with inner delight, opening and shutting its lips, its body large and rigid with excitement. Yet it never for one instant paused in its short journeys to and fro.

He noted exactly what it did: it walked, he saw, the same number of paces each time, some six or seven steps, and then it turned sharply and retraced them. By the pattern of the great roses in the carpet he measured it. It kept the same direction and the same line. It behaved precisely as though it were rubbing against something solid. Undoubtedly there was something standing there on that strip of carpet, something invisible to the doctor, something that alarmed the dog, yet caused the cat unspeakable pleasure.

'Smokie!' he called again, 'Smokie, you black mystery, what is it excites you so?'

Again the cat looked up at him for a brief second, and then continued its sentry-walk, blissfully happy, intensely preoccupied. And, for an instant, as he watched it, the doctor was aware that a faint uneasiness stirred in the depths of his own being, focusing itself for the moment upon this curious behaviour of the uncanny creature before him.

There rose in him quite a new realisation of the mystery connected with the whole feline tribe, but especially with that common member of it, the domestic cat – their hidden lives, their strange aloofness, their incalculable subtlety. How utterly remote from anything that human beings understood lay the sources of their elusive activities. As he watched the indescribable bearing of the little creature mincing along the strip of carpet under his eyes, coquetting with the powers of darkness, welcoming, maybe, some fearsome visitor, there stirred in his heart a feeling strangely akin to awe. Its indifference to human kind, its serene superiority to the obvious, struck him forcibly with fresh meaning; so remote, so inaccessible seemed the secret purposes of its real life, so alien to the blundering honesty of other animals. Its absolute poise of bearing brought into his mind the opium-eater's words that 'no dignity is perfect which does not at some point ally itself with the mysterious'; and he became suddenly aware that the presence of the dog in this foggy, haunted room on the top of Putney Hill was uncommonly welcome to him. He was glad to feel that Flame's dependable personality was with him. The savage growling at his heels was a pleasant sound. He was glad to hear it. That marching cat made him uneasy.

Finding that Smoke paid no further attention to his words, the doctor decided upon action. Would it rub against his leg, too? He would take it by surprise and see.

He stepped quickly forward and placed himself upon

- the exact strip of carpet where it walked.

But no cat is ever taken by surprise! The moment he occupied the space of the Intruder, setting his feet on the woven roses midway in the line of travel, Smoke suddenly stopped purring and sat down. It lifted up its face with the most innocent stare imaginable of its green eyes. He could have sworn it laughed. It was a perfect child again. In a single second it had resumed its simple, domestic manner; and it gazed at him in such a way that he almost felt Smoke was the normal being, and *his* was the eccentric behaviour that was being watched. It was consummate, the manner in which it brought about this change so easily and so quickly.

'Superb little actor!' he laughed in spite of himself, and stooped to stroke the shining black back. But, in a flash, as he touched its fur, the cat turned and spat at him viciously, striking at his hand with one paw. Then, with a hurried scutter of feet, it shot like a shadow across the floor, and a moment later was calmly sitting over by the window-curtains washing its face as though nothing interested it in the whole world but the cleanness of its cheeks and whiskers.

John Silence straightened himself up and drew a long breath. He realised that the performance was temporarily at an end. The collie, meanwhile, who had watched the whole proceeding with marked disapproval, had now lain down again upon the mat by the fire, no longer growling. It seemed to the doctor just as though something had entered the room while he slept, alarming the dog, yet bringing happiness to the cat, had now gone out again, leaving all as it was before. Whatever it was that excited its blissful attentions had retreated for the moment.

He realised this intuitively. Smoke evidently realised it, too, for presently he deigned to march back to the fireplace and jump upon his master's knees. Dr Silence, patient and determined, settled down once more to his book. The animals soon slept; the fire blazed cheerfully; and the cold fog from outside poured into the room through every available chink and cranny.

For a long time silence and peace reigned in the room and Dr Silence availed himself of the quietness to make careful notes of what had happened. He entered for future use in other cases an exhaustive analysis of what he had observed, especially with regard to the effect upon the two animals. It is impossible here, nor would it be intelligible to the reader unversed in the knowledge of the region known to a scientifically trained psychic like Dr Silence, to detail these observations. But to him it was clear, up to a certain point – and for the rest he must still wait and watch. So far, at least, he realised that while he slept in the chair – that is, while his will was dormant – the room had suffered intrusion from what he recognised as an intensely active Force, and might later be forced to acknowledge as something more than merely a blind force, namely, a distinct personality.

So far it had affected himself scarcely at all, but had acted directly upon the simpler organisms of the animals. It stimulated keenly the centres of the cat's psychic being, inducing a stare of instant happiness (intensifying its consciousness probably in the same way a drug or stimulant intensifies that of a human being); whereas it alarmed the less sensitive dog, causing it to feel a vague apprehension and distress.

His own sudden action and exhibition of energy had served to disperse it temporarily, yet he felt convinced – the indications were not lacking even while he sat there making notes – that it still remained near to him, conditionally if not spatially, and was, as it were, gathering force for a second attack.

And, further, he intuitively understood that the relations between the two animals had undergone a subtle change: that the cat had become immeasurably superior, confident, sure of itself in its own peculiar region, whereas Flame had been weakened by an attack he could not comprehend and knew not how to reply to. Though not yet afraid, he was defiant – ready to act against a fear that he felt to be approaching. He was no longer fatherly and protective towards the cat. Smoke held the key to the situation; and both he and the cat knew it.

Thus, as the minutes passed, John Silence sat and waited, keenly on the alert, wondering how soon the attack would be renewed, and at what point it would be diverted from the animals and directed upon himself.

The book lay on the floor beside him, his notes were

complete. With one hand on the cat's fur, and the dog's front paws resting against his feet, the three of them dozed comfortably before the hot fire while the night wore on and the silence deepened towards midnight.

It was well after one o'clock in the morning when Dr Silence turned the lamp out and lighted the candle preparatory to going up to bed. Then Smoke suddenly woke with a loud sharp purr and sat up. It neither stretched, washed nor turned: it listened. And the doctor, watching it, realised that a certain indefinable change had come about that very moment in the room. A swift readjustment of the forces within the four walls had taken place – a new disposition of their personal equations. The balance was destroyed, the former harmony gone. Smoke, most sensitive of barometers, had been the first to feel it, but the dog was not slow to follow suit, for on looking down he noted that Flame was no longer asleep. He was lying with eyes wide open, and that same instant he sat up on his great haunches and began to growl.

Dr Silence was in the act of taking the matches to re-light the lamp when an audible movement in the room behind made him pause. Smoke leaped down from his knee and moved forward a few paces across the carpet. Then it stopped and stared fixedly; and the doctor stood up on the rug to watch.

As he rose the sound was repeated, and he discovered that it was not in the room as he first thought, but outside, and that it came from more directions than one. There was a rushing, sweeping noise against the window-panes, and simultaneously a sound of something brushing against the door – out in the hall. Smoke advanced sedately across the carpet, twitching his tail, and sat down within a foot of the door. The influence that had destroyed the harmonious conditions of the room had apparently moved in advance of its cause. Clearly, something was about to happen.

For the first time that night John Silence hesitated; the thought of that dark narrow hall-way, choked with fog, and destitute of human comfort, was unpleasant. He became aware of a faint creeping of his flesh. He knew, of course, that the actual opening of the door was not necessary to the invasion of the room that was about to take place, since neither doors nor windows, nor any other solid barriers would interpose an obstacle to what was seeking entrance. Yet the opening of the door would be significant and symbolic, and he distinctly shrank from it.

But for a moment only. Smoke, turning with a show of impatience, recalled him to his purpose, and he moved past the sitting, watching creature, and deliberately opened the door to its full width.

What subsequently happened, happened in the feeble and flickering light of the solitary candle on the mantelpiece.

Through the open door he saw the hall, dimly lit and thick with fog. Nothing, of course, was visible – nothing but the hat-stand, and African spears in dark lines upon the wall and the high-backed wooden chair standing grotesquely underneath on the oilcloth floor. For one instant the fog seemed to move and thicken oddly; but he set that down to the score of the imagination. The door had opened upon nothing.

Yet Smoke apparently thought otherwise, and the deep growling of the collie from the mat at the back of the room seemed to confirm his judgement.

For, proud and self-possessed, the cat had again risen to his feet, and having advanced to the door, was now ushering someone slowly into the room. Nothing could have been more evident. He paced from side to side, bowing his little head with great *empressement* and holding his stiffened tail aloft like a flagstaff. He turned this way and that, mincing to and fro, and showing signs of supreme satisfaction. He was in his element. He welcomed the intrusion, and apparently reckoned that his companions, the doctor and the dog, would welcome it likewise.

The Intruder had returned for a second attack.

Dr Silence moved slowly backward and took up his position on the hearthrug, keying himself up to a condition of concentrated attention.

He noted that Flame stood beside him, facing the room, with body motionless, and head moving swiftly from side to side with a curious swaying movement. His eyes were wide open, his back rigid, his neck and jaws thrust forward, his legs tense and ready to leap. Savage, ready for attack or defence, yet dreadfully puzzled and perhaps already a little cowed, he stood and stared, the hair on his spine and sides positively bristling outwards as though a wind played through them. In the dim firelight he looked like a great yellow-haired wolf, silent, eyes shooting dark fire, exceedingly formidable. It was Flame, the terrible.

Smoke, meanwhile, advanced from the door towards the middle of the room, adopting the very slow pace of an invisible companion. A few feet away it stopped and began to smile and blink its eyes. There was something deliberately coaxing in its attitude as it stood there undecided on the carpet, clearly wishing to effect some sort of introduction between the Intruder and its canine friend and ally. It assumed its most winning manners, purring, smiling, looking persuasively from one to the other, and making quick tentative steps first in one direction and then in the other. There had always existed such perfect understanding between them in everything. Surely Flame would appreciate Smoke's intentions now, and acquiesce.

But the old collie made no advances. He bared his teeth, lifting his lips till the gums showed, and stood stockstill with fixed eyes and heaving sides. The doctor moved a little farther back, watching intently the smallest movement, and it was just then he divined suddenly from the cat's behaviour and attitude that it was not only a single companion it had ushered into the room, but *several*. It kept crossing over from one to the other, looking up at each in turn. It sought to win over the dog to friendliness with them all. The original Intruder had come back with reinforcements. And at the same time he further realised that the Intruder was something more than a blindly acting force, impersonal though destructive. It was a Personality, and moreover a great personality. And it was accompanied for the purposes of assistance by a host of other personalities, minor in degree, but similar in kind.

He braced himself in the corner against the mantelpiece and waited, his whole being roused to defence, for he was now fully aware that the attack had spread to include himself as well as the animals, and he must be on the alert. He strained his eyes through the foggy atmosphere, trying in vain to see what the cat and dog saw; but the candlelight threw an uncertain and flickering light across the room and his eyes discerned nothing. On the floor Smoke moved softly in front of him like a black shadow, his eyes gleaming as he turned his head, still trying with many insinuating gestures and much purring to bring about the introductions he desired.

But it was all in vain. Flame stood riveted to one spot, motionless as a figure carved in stone.

Some minutes passed, during which only the cat moved, and then there came a sharp change. Flame began to back towards the wall. He moved his head from side to side as he went, sometimes turning to snap at something almost behind him. *They* were advancing upon him, trying to surround him. His distress became very marked from now onwards, and it seemed to the doctor that his anger merged into genuine terror and became overwhelmed by it. The savage growl sounded perilously like a whine, and more than once he tried to dive past his master's legs, as though hunting for a way of escape. He was trying to avoid something that everywhere blocked the way.

This terror of the indomitable fighter impressed the doctor enormously; yet also painfully; stirring his impatience; for he had never before seen the dog show signs of giving in, and it distressed him to witness it. He knew, however, that he was not giving in easily, and understood that it was really impossible for him to gauge the animal's sensations properly at all. What Flame felt, and saw, must be terrible indeed to turn him all at once into a coward. He faced something that made him afraid of more than his life merely. The doctor spoke a few quick words of encouragement to him, and stroked the bristling hair. But without much success. The collie seemed already beyond the reach of comfort such as that, and the collapse of the old dog followed indeed very speedily after this.

And Smoke, meanwhile, remained behind, watching the advance, but not joining in it; sitting, pleased and expectant, considering that all was going well and as it wished. It was kneading on the carpet with its front paws – slowly, laboriously, as though its feet were dipped in treacle. The sound its claws made as they caught in the threads was distinctly audible. It was still smiling, blinking, purring.

Suddenly the collie uttered a poignant short bark and leaped heavily to one side. His bared teeth traced a line of whiteness through the gloom. The next instant he dashed past his master's legs, almost upsetting his balance, and shot out into the room, where he went blundering wildly against walls and furniture. But that bark was significant; the doctor had heard it before and knew what it meant; for it was the cry of the fighter against odds and it meant that the old beast had found his courage again. Possibly it was only the courage of despair, but at any rate the fighting would be terrific. And Dr Silence understood, too, that he dared not interfere. Flame must fight his own enemies in his own way.

But the cat, too, had heard that dreadful bark; and it, too, had understood. This was more than it had bargained for. Across the dim shadows of that haunted room there must have passed some secret signal of distress between the animals. Smoke stood up and looked swiftly about him. He uttered a piteous meow and trotted smartly away into the greater darkness by the windows. What his object was only those endowed with the spirit-like intelligence of cats might know. But, at any rate, he had at last ranged himself on the side of his friend. And the little beast meant business.

At the same moment the collie managed to gain the door. The doctor saw him rush through into the hall like a flash of yellow light. He shot across the oilcloth, and tore up the stairs, but in another second he appeared again, flying down the steps and landing at the bottom in a tumbling heap, whining, cringing, terrified. The doctor saw him slink back into the room again and crawl round by the wall towards the cat. Was, then, even the staircase occupied? Did *they* stand also in the hall? Was the whole house crowded from floor to ceiling?

The thought came to add to the keen distress he felt at the sight of the collie's discomfiture. And, indeed, his own personal distress had increased in a marked degree during the past minutes, and continued to increase steadily to the climax. He recognised that the drain on his own vitality grew steadily, and that the attack was now directed against himself even more than against the defeated dog, and the too much deceived cat.

It all seemed so rapid and uncalculated after that – the events that took place in this little modern room at the top of Putney Hill between midnight and sunrise – that Dr Silence was hardly able to follow and remember it all. It came about with such uncanny swiftness and terror; the light was so uncertain; the movements of the black cat so difficult to follow on the dark carpet, and the doctor himself so weary and taken by surprise – that he found it almost impossible to observe accurately, or to recall afterwards precisely what it was he had seen or in what order the incidents had taken place. He never could understand what defect of vision on his part made it seem as though the cat had duplicated itself at first, and then increased indefinitely, so that there were at least a dozen of them darting silently about the floor, leaping softly on to chairs and tables, passing like shadows from the open door to the end of the room, all black as sin, with brilliant green eyes flashing fire in all directions. It was like the reflections from a score of mirrors placed round the walls at different angles. Nor could he make out at the time why the size of the room seemed to have altered, grown much larger, and why it extended away behind him where ordinarily the wall should have been. The snarling of the enraged and terrified collie sounded sometimes so far away; the ceiling seemed to have raised itself so much higher than before, and much of the furniture had changed in appearance and shifted marvellously.

It was all so confused and confusing, as though the little room he knew had become merged and transformed into the dimensions of quite another chamber, that came to him, with the host of cats and its strange distances, in a sort of vision.

But these changes came about a little later, and at a time when his attention was so concentrated upon the proceedings of Smoke and the collie, that he only observed them, as it were, subconsciously. And the excitement, the flickering candlelight, the distress he felt for the collie, and the distorting atmosphere of fog were the poorest possible allies to careful observation.

At first he was only aware that the dog was repeating his short dangerous bark from time to time, snapping viciously at the empty air, a foot or so from the ground. Once, indeed, he sprang upwards and forwards, working furiously with teeth and paws, and with a noise like wolves fighting, but only to dash back the next minute against the wall behind him. Then, after lying still for a bit, he rose to a crouching position as though to spring again, snarling horribly and making short half-circles with lowered head. And Smoke all the while meowed piteously by the window as though trying to draw the attack upon himself.

Then it was that the rush of the whole dreadful business seemed to turn aside from the dog and direct itself upon his own person. The collie had made another spring and fallen back with a crash into the corner, where he made noise enough in his savage rage to waken the dead before he fell to whining and then finally lay still. And directly afterwards the doctor's own distress became intolerably acute. He had made a half movement forward to come to the rescue when a veil that was denser than mere fog seemed to drop down over the scene, draping room, walls, animals and fire in a mist of darkness and folding also about his own mind. Other forms moved silently across the field of vision, forms that he recognised from previous experiments, and welcomed not. Unholy thoughts began to crowd into his brain, sinister suggestions of evil presented themselves seductively. Ice seemed to settle about his heart, and his mind trembled. He began to lose memory — memory of his identity, of where he was, of what he ought to do. The very foundations of his strength were shaken. His will seemed paralysed.

And it was then that the room filled with this horde of cats, all dark as the night, all silent, all with lamping eyes of green fire. The dimensions of the place altered and shifted. He was in a much larger space. The whining of the dog sounded far away, and all about him the cats flew busily to and fro, silently playing their tearing, rushing game of evil, weaving the pattern of their dark purpose upon the floor. He strove hard to collect himself and remember the words of power he had made use of before in similar dread positions where his dangerous practice had sometimes led; but he could recall nothing consecutively; a mist lay over his mind and memory; he felt dazed and his forces scattered. The deeps within were too troubled for healing power to come out of them.

It was glamour, of course, he realised afterwards, the strong glamour thrown upon his imagination by some powerful personality behind the veil; but at the time he was not sufficiently aware of this and, as with all true glamour, was unable to grasp where the true ended and the false began. He was caught momentarily in the same vortex that had sought to lure the cat to destruction through its delight, and threatened utterly to overwhelm the dog through its terror.

There came a sound in the chimney behind him like wind booming and tearing its way down. The windows rattled. The candle flickered and went out. The glacial atmosphere closed round him with the cold of death, and a great rushing sound swept by overhead as though the ceiling had lifted to a great height. He heard the door shut. Far away it sounded. He felt lost, shelterless in the depths of his soul. Yet still he held out and resisted while the climax of the fight came nearer and nearer. ... He had stepped into the stream of forces awakened by Pender, and he knew that he must withstand them to the end or come to a conclusion that it was not good for a man to come to. Something from the region of utter cold was upon him.

And then quite suddenly, through the confused mists about him, there slowly rose up the Personality that had been all the time directing the battle. Some force entered his being that shook him as the tempest shakes a leaf, and close against his eyes – clean level with his face – he found himself staring into the wreck of a vast dark Countenance, a countenance that was terrible even in its ruin.

For ruined it was, and terrible it was, and the mark of spiritual evil was branded everywhere upon its broken features. Eyes, face, and hair rose level with his own, and for a space of time he never could properly measure, or determine, these two, a man and a woman, looked straight into each other's visages and down into each other's hearts.

And John Silence, the soul with the good, unselfish motive, held his own against the dark discarnate woman whose motive was pure evil, and whose soul was on the side of the Dark Powers.

It was the climax that touched the depth of power within him and began to restore him slowly to his own. He was conscious, of course, of effort, and yet it seemed no super-human one, for he had recognised the character of his opponent's power, and he called upon the good within him to meet and overcome it. The inner forces stirred and trembled in response to his call. They did not at first come readily as was their habit, for under the spell of glamour they had already been diabolically lulled into inactivity, but come they eventually did, rising out of the inner spiritual nature he had learned with so much time and pain to awaken to life. And power and confidence came with them. He began to breathe deeply and regularly, and at the same time to absorb into himself the forces opposed to him, and to *turn them to his own account*. By ceasing to resist, and allowing the deadly stream to pour into him unopposed, he used the very power supplied by his adversary and thus enormously increased his own.

For this spiritual alchemy he had learned. He understood that force ultimately is everywhere one and the same; it is the motive behind that makes it good or evil; and his motive was entirely unselfish. He knew – provided he was not first robbed of self-control – how vicariously to absorb these evil radiations into himself and change them magically into his own good purposes. And, since his motive was pure and his soul fearless, they could not work him harm.

Thus he stood in the main stream of evil unwittingly attracted by Pender, deflecting its course upon himself; and after passing through the purifying filter of his own unselfishness these energies could only add to his store of experience, of knowledge, and therefore of power. And, as his self-control returned to him, he gradually accomplished this purpose, even though trembling while he did so.

Yet the struggle was severe, and in spite of the freezing chill of the air, the perspiration poured down his face. Then, by slow degrees, the dark and dreadful countenance faded, the glamour passed from his soul, the normal proportions returned to walls and ceiling, the forms melted back into the fog, and the whirl of rushing shadow-cats disappeared whence they came.

And with the return of the consciousness of his own identity John Silence was restored to the full control of his own will-power. In a deep, modulated voice he began to utter certain rhythmical sounds that slowly rolled through the air like a rising sea, filling the room with powerful vibratory activities that whelmed all irregularities of lesser vibrations in its own swelling tone. He made certain sigils, gestures, and movements at the same time. For several minutes he continued to utter these words, until at length the growing volume dominated the whole room and mastered the manifestation of all that opposed it. For just as he understood the spiritual alchemy that can transmute evil forces by raising them into higher channels, so he knew from long study the occult use of sound, and its direct effect upon the plastic region wherein the powers of spiritual evil work their fell purposes. Harmony was restored first of all to his own soul, and thence to the room and all its occupants.

And, after himself, the first to recognise it was the old dog lying in his corner. Flame began suddenly uttering sounds of pleasure that 'something' between a growl and a grunt that dogs make upon being restored to their master's confidence. Dr Silence heard the thumping of the collie's tail against the ground. And the grunt and the thumping touched the depth of affection in the man's heart, and gave him some inkling of what agonies the dumb creature had suffered.

Next, from the shadows by the window, a somewhat shrill purring announced the restoration of the cat to its normal state. Smoke was advancing across the carpet. He seemed very pleased with himself, and smiled with an expression of supreme innocence. He was no shadow-cat, but real and full of his usual and perfect self-possession. He marched along, picking his way delicately, but with a stately dignity that suggested his ancestry with the majesty of Egypt. His eyes no longer glared; they shone steadily before him; they radiated, not excitement, but knowledge. Clearly he was anxious to make amends for the mischief to which he had unwittingly lent himself owing to his subtle and electric constitution.

Still uttering his sharp high purrings he marched up to his master and rubbed vigorously against his legs. Then he stood on his hind feet and pawed his knees and stared beseechingly up into his face. He turned his head towards the corner where the collie still lay, thumping his tail feebly and pathetically.

John Silence understood. He bent down and stroked the creature's living fur, noting the line of bright blue sparks that followed the motion of his hand down its back. And then they advanced together towards the corner where the dog was.

Smoke went first and put his nose gently against his friend's muzzle, purring while he rubbed, and uttering little soft sounds of affection in his throat. The doctor lit the candle and brought it over. He saw the collie lying on its side against the wall; it was utterly exhausted, and foam still hung about its jaws. Its tail and eyes responded to the sound of its name, but it was evidently very weak and overcome. Smoke continued to rub against its cheeks and nose and eyes, sometimes even standing on its body and kneading into the thick yellow hair. Flame replied from time to time by little licks of the tongue, most of them curiously misdirected.

But Dr Silence felt intuitively that something disastrous had happened, and his heart was wrung. He stroked the dear body, feeling it over for bruises or broken bones, but finding none. He fed it with what remained of the sandwiches and milk, but the creature clumsily upset the saucer and lost the sandwiches between its paws, so that the doctor had to feed it with his own hand. And all the while Smoke meowed piteously.

Then John Silence began to understand. He went across to the farther side of the room and called aloud to it.

'Flame, old man! come!'

At any other time the dog would have been upon him in an instant, barking and leaping to the shoulder. And even now he got up, though heavily and awkwardly, to his feet. He started to run, waging his tail more briskly. He collided

67

first with a chair, and then ran straight into a table. Smoke trotted close at his side, trying his very best to guide him. But it was useless. Dr Silence had to lift him up into his own arms and carry him like a baby. For he was blind.

<h1 style="text-align:center">3</h1>

IT WAS a week later when John Silence called to see the author in his new house, and found him well on the way to recovery, and already busy again with his writing. The haunted look had left his eyes, and he seemed cheerful and confident.

'Humour restored?' laughed the doctor as soon as they were comfortably settled in the room overlooking the Park.

'I've had no trouble since I left that dreadful place,' returned Pender gratefully; 'and thanks to you —'

The doctor stopped him with a gesture.

'Never mind that,' he said, 'we'll discuss your new plans afterwards, and my scheme for relieving you of the house and helping you settle elsewhere. Of course it must be pulled down, for it's not fit for any sensitive person to live in, and any other tenant might be afflicted in the same way you were. Although, personally, I think the evil has exhausted itself by now.'

He told the astonished author something of his experiences in it with the animals.

'I don't pretend to understand,' Pender said, when the account was finished, 'but I and my wife are intensely relieved to be free of it all. Only I must say I should like to know something of the former history of the house. When we took it six months ago I heard no word against it.'

Dr Silence drew a typewritten paper from his pocket.

'I can satisfy your curiosity to some extent,' he said, running his eye over the sheets, and then replacing them in his coat; 'for by my secretary's investigations I have been able to check certain information obtained in the hypnotic trance by a "sensitive" who helps me in such cases. The former occupant who haunted you appears to have been a woman of singularly atrocious life and character who finally suffered death by hanging, after a series of crimes that appalled the whole of England and only came to light by the merest chance. She came to her end in the year 1798, for it was not this particular house she lived in, but a much larger one that then stood upon the site it now occupies, and was then, of course, not in London, but in the country. She was a person of intellect, possessed of a powerful, trained will, and of consummate audacity, and I am convinced availed herself of the resources of the lower magic to attain her ends. This goes far to explain the virulence of the attack upon yourself, and why she is still able to carry on after death the evil practices that formed her main purpose during life.'

'You think that after death a soul can still consciously direct —' gasped the author.

'I think, as I told you before, that the forces of a powerful personality may still persist after death in the line of their original momentum,' replied the doctor; 'and that strong thoughts and purposes can still react upon suitably prepared brains long after their originators have passed away.

'If you knew anything of magic,' he pursued, 'you would know that thought is dynamic, and that it may call into existence forms and pictures that may well exist for hundreds of years. For, not far removed from the region of our human life, is another region where floats the waste and drift of all the centuries, the limbo of the shells of the dead; a densely populated region crammed with horror and abomination of all descriptions, and sometimes galvanised into active life again by the will of a trained manipulator, a mind versed in the practices of lower magic. That this woman understood its vile commerce, I am persuaded, and the forces she set going during her life have simply been accumulating ever since, and would have continued to do so had they not been drawn down upon yourself, and afterwards discharged and satisfied through me.

'Anything might have brought down the attack, for, besides drugs, there are certain violent emotions, certain moods of the soul, certain spiritual fevers, if I may so call them, which directly open the inner being to a cognisance of this astral region I have mentioned. In your case it happened to be a peculiarly potent drug that did it.

'But now tell me,' he added, after a pause, handing to the

perplexed author a pencil-drawing he had made of the dark countenance that had appeared to him during the night on Putney Hill – 'tell me if you recognise this face?'

Pender looked at the drawing closely, greatly astonished. He shuddered a little as he looked.

'Undoubtedly,' he said, 'it is the face I kept trying to draw – dark, with the great mouth and jaw, and the drooping eye. That is the woman.'

Dr Silence then produced from his pocket-book an old-fashioned woodcut of the same person which his secretary had unearthed from the records of the Newgate Calendar. The woodcut and the pencil drawing were two different aspects of the same dreadful visage. The men compared them for some moments in silence.

'It makes me thank God for the limitations of our senses,' said Pender, with a sigh; 'continuous clairvoyance must be a sore affliction.'

'It is indeed,' returned John Silence significantly, 'and if all the people nowadays who claim to be clairvoyant were really so, the statistics of suicide and lunacy would be considerably higher than they are. It is little wonder,' he added, 'that your sense of humour was clouded, with the mind-forces of that dead monster trying to use your brain for their dissemination. You have had an interesting adventure, Mr Felix Pender, and, let me add, a fortunate escape.'

The author was about to renew his thanks when there came a sound of scratching at the door, and the doctor sprang up quickly.

'It's time for me to go. I left my dog on the step, but I suppose —'

Before he had time to open the door, it had yielded to the pressure behind it and flew wide open to admit a great yellow-haired collie. The dog, wagging his tail and contorting his whole body with delight, tore across the floor and tried to leap up upon his owner's breast. And there was laughter and happiness in the old eyes; for they were clear again as the day.

The Old Man of Visions

I

THE IMAGE of Teufelsdröckh, sitting in his watch-tower 'alone with stars,' leaped into my mind the moment I saw him; and the curious expression of his eyes proclaimed at once that here was a being who allowed the world of small effects to pass him by, while he himself dwelt among the eternal verities. It was only necessary to catch a glimpse of the bent grey figure, so slight yet so tremendous, to realise that he carried staff and wallet, and was travelling alone in a spiritual region, uncharted, and full of wonder, difficulty, and fearful joy.

The inner eye perceived this quite as clearly as the outer was aware of his Hebraic ancestry; but along what winding rivers, through what haunted woods, by the shores of what singing seas he pressed forward towards the mountains of his goal, no one could guess from a mere inspection of that wonderful old face.

To have stumbled upon such a figure in the casual way I did seemed incredible to me even at the time, yet I at once caught something of the uplifting airs that followed this inhabitant of a finer world, and I spent days – and considered them well spent – trying to get into conversation with him, so that I might know something more than the thin disguise of his holding a reader's ticket for the Museum Library.

To reach the stage of intimacy where actual speech is a hindrance to close understanding, one need not in some cases have spoken at all; thus by merely setting my mind, and above all, my imagination, into tune with his and by steeping myself so much in his atmosphere that I absorbed and then gave back to him with my own stamp the forces he exhaled, it was at length possible to persuade those vast-seeing eyes to turn in my direction; and our glances having once met, I simply rose when he rose, and followed him out of the little smoky restaurant so closely up the street that our clothes brushed, and I thought I could even catch the sound of his breathing.

Whether, having already weighed me, he accepted the office, or whether he was grateful for the arm to lean upon, with his many years' burden, I do not know; but the sympathy between us was such that, without a single word, we walked up that foggy London street to the door of his lodging in Bloomsbury, while I noticed that at the touch of his arm the noise of the town seemed to turn into deep singing, and even the hurrying passers-by seemed bent upon noble purposes; and though he barely reached to my shoulder, and his grey beard almost touched my glove as I bent my arm to hold his own, there was something immense about his figure that sent him with towering stature above me and filled my thoughts with enchanting dreams of grandeur and high beauty.

But it was only when the door had closed on him with a little rush of wind, and I was walking home alone, that I fully realised the shock of my return to earth; and on reaching my own rooms I shook with laughter to think I had walked a mile and a half with a complete stranger without uttering a single syllable. Then the laughter suddenly hushed as I caught my face in the glass with the expression of the soul still lingering about the eyes and forehead, and for a brief moment my heart leaped to a sort of noble fever in the blood, leaving me with the smart of the soul's wings stirring beneath the body's crushing weight. And when it passed I found myself dwelling upon the only words he had spoken when I left him at the door:

'I am the Old Man of Visions, and I am *at your service.*'

I think he never had a name – at least, it never passed his lips, and perhaps lay buried with so much else of the past that he clearly deemed unimportant. To me, at any rate, he became simply the Old Man of Visions, and to the little waiting-maid and the old landlady he was known simply as 'Mister' – Mister, neither more nor less. The impenetrable veil that hung over his past never lifted for any vital revelations of his personal history, though he evidently knew all countries of the world, and had absorbed into his heart and brain the experience of all possible types of human nature; and there was an air about him not so much of 'Ask me no questions,' as 'Do not ask me, for I cannot answer you *in words.*'

He could satisfy, but not in mere language; he would reveal, but by the wonderful words of silence only; for he was the Old Man of Visions, and visions need no words, being swift and of the spirit.

Moreover, the landlady – poor, dusty, faded woman – the landlady stood in awe, and disliked being probed for information in a passage-way down which he might any moment tread, for she could only tell me, 'He just came in one night, years ago, and he's been here ever since!' And more than that I never knew. 'Just came in – one night – years ago.' This adequately explained him, for where he came *from*, or was journeying *to*, was something quite beyond the scope of ordinary limited language.

I pictured him suddenly turning aside from the stream of unimportant events, quietly stepping out of the world of straining, fighting, and shouting, and moving to take his rightful place among the forces of the still, spiritual region where he belonged by virtue of long pain and difficult attainment. For he was unconnected with any conceivable network of relations, friends, or family, and his terrible aloofness could not be disturbed by anyone unless with his permission and by his express wish. Nor could he be imagined as 'belonging' to any definite set of souls. He was apart from the world – and above it.

But it was only when I began to creep a little nearer to him, and our strange, silent intimacy passed from mental to spiritual, that I began really to understand more of this wonderful Old Man of Visions.

Steeped in the tragedy, and convulsed with laughter at the comedy, of life, he yet lived there in his high attic wrapped in silence as in a golden cloud; and so seldom did he actually speak to me that each time the sound of his voice, that had something elemental in it – something of winds and waters – thrilled me with the power of the first time.

He lived, like Teufelsdröckh, 'alone with the stars,' and it seemed impossible, more and more, to link him on anywhere into practical dealings with ordinary men and women. Life somehow seemed to pass *below* him. Yet the small, selfish spirit of the recluse was far from him, and he was tenderly and deeply responsive to pain and suffering, and more particularly to genuine yearning for the far things of beauty. The unsatisfied longings of others could move him at once to tears.

'My relations with men are perfect,' he said one night as we neared his dwelling. 'I give them all sympathy out of my stores of knowledge and experience, and they give to me what kindness I need. My outer shell lies within impenetrable solitude, for only so can my inner life move freely along the paths and terraces that are thronged with the beings to whom I belong.' And when I asked him how he maintained such deep sympathy with humanity, and had yet absolved himself apparently from action as from speech, he stopped against an area railing and turned his great eyes on to my face, as though their fires could communicate his thought without the husk of words:

'I have peered too profoundly into life and beyond it,' he murmured, 'to wish to express in language what I *know*. Action is not for all, always; and I am in touch with the cisterns of thought that lie behind action. I ponder the mysteries. What I may solve is not lost for lack either of speech or action, for the true mystic is ever the true man of action, and my thought will reach others as soon as they are ready for it in the same way that it reached you. All who strongly yearn must, sooner or later, find me and be comforted.'

His eyes shifted from my face towards the stars, softly shining above the dark Museum roof, and a moment later he had disappeared into the hall-way of his house.

'An old poet who has strayed afield and lost his way,' I mused; but through the door where he had just vanished came back to me as from a great distance: 'A priest, rather, who has begun to find his way.'

For a space I stood, pondering on his face and words – that mercilessly intelligent look of the Hebrew woven in with the expression of the sadness of a whole race, yet touched with the glory of the spirit; and his utterance – that he had passed through all the traditions and no longer needed a formal, limited creed to hold to. I forget how I reached my own door several miles away, but it seemed to me that I flew.

In this way, and by unregistered degrees, we came to know each other better, and he accepted me and took me into his life. Always wrapped in the great calm of his delightful silence, he taught me more, and told me more, than could ever lie within the confines of mere words; and in moments of need, no matter when or where, I always knew exactly how to find him, reaching him in a few seconds by some swift way that disdained the means of ordinary locomotion.

Then at last one day he gave me the key of his house. And the first time I found my way into his aerie, and realised that it was a haven I could always fly to when the yearnings of the heart and soul struggled vainly for recompense, the full meaning and importance of the Old Man of Visions became finally clear to me.

2

The room, high up creaky, darkened stairs, in the ancient house, was bare and fireless, looking through a single patched window across a tumbled sea of roofs and chimneys; yet there was that in it which instantly proclaimed it a little holy place out of the world, a temple in which someone with spiritual vitality had worshipped, prayed, wept, and sung.

It was dusty and unswept, yet it was utterly *unsoiled*; and the Old Man of Visions who lived there, for all his shabby and stained garments, his uncombed beard and broken shoes, stood within its door revealed in his real self, moving in a sort of divine whiteness, iridescent, shining. And here, in this attic (lampless and unswept), high up under the old roofs of Bloomsbury, the window scarred with rain and the corners dropping cobwebs, I heard his silver whisper issue from the shadows:

'Here you may satisfy your soul's desire and may commune with the Invisibles; only, to find the Invisibles, you

75

must first be able to lose yourself.'

Ah! through that stained window-pane, the sight leaping at a single bound from black roofs up to the stars, what pictures, dreams, and visions the Old Man has summoned to my eyes! Distances, measureless and impossible hitherto, became easy, and from the oppression of dead bricks and the market-place he transported me in a moment to the slopes of the Mountains of Dream; leading me to little places near the summits where the pines grew thinly and the stars were visible through their branches, fading into the rose of dawn; where the winds tasted of the desert, and the voices of the wilderness fled upward with a sound of wings and falling streams. At his word houses melted away, and the green waves of all the seas flowed into their places; forests waved themselves into the coastline of dull streets; and the power of the old earth, with all her smells and flowers and wild life, thrilled down among the dead roofs and caught me away into freedom among the sunshine of meadows and the music of sweet pipings. And with the divine deliverance came the crying of sea-gulls, the glimmer of reedy tarns, the whispering of wind among grasses, and the healing scorch of a real sun upon the skin.

And poetry such as was never known or heard before clothed all he uttered, yet even then took no form in actual words, for it was of the substance of aspiration and yearning, voicing adequately all the busy, high-born dreams that haunt the soul yet never live in the uttered line. He breathed it about him in the air so that it filled my being. It was part of him – beyond words; and it sang my own longings, and sang them perfectly so that I was satisfied; for my own mood never failed to touch him instantly and to waken the right response. In its essence it was spiritual – the mystic poetry of heaven; still, the love of humanity informed it, for star-fire and heart's blood were about equally mingled there, while the mystery of unattainable beauty moved through it like a white flame.

With other dreams and longings, too, it was the same; and all the most beautiful ideas that ever haunted a soul unendowed with expression here floated with satisfied eyes and smiling lips before one – floated in silence, unencumbered, unlimited, unrestrained by words.

In this dim room, never made ugly by artificial light, but always shadowy in a kind of gentle dusk, the Old Man of Visions had only to lead me to the window to bring peace. Music, that rendered the soul fluid, as it poured across the old roofs into the room, was summoned by him at need; and when one's wings beat sometimes against the prison walls and the yearning for escape oppressed the heart, I have heard the little room rush and fill with the sound of trees, wind among grasses, whispering branches, and lapping waters. The very odours of space and mountain-side came too, and the looming of noble hills seemed visible overhead against the stars, as though the ceiling had suddenly become transparent.

For the Old Man of Visions had the power of instantly satisfying an ideal when once that ideal created a yearning that could tear and burn its way out with sufficient force to set the will a-moving.

3

BUT AS the time passed and I came to depend more and more upon the intimacy with my strange old friend, new light fell upon the nature and possibilities of our connection. I discovered, for instance, that though I held the key to his dwelling, and was familiar with the way, he was nevertheless not always available. Two things, in different fashion, rendered him inaccessible, or mute; and, for the first, I gradually learned that when life was prosperous, and the body singing loud, I could not find my way to his house. No amount of wandering, calculation, or persevering effort enabled me even to find the street again. With any burst of worldly success, however fleeting, the Old Man of Vision somehow slipped away into remote shadows and became unreal and misty. A merely passing desire to be with him, to seek his inspiration by a glimpse through that magic window-pane, resulted only in vain and tiresome pacing to and fro along ugly streets that produced weariness and depression; and after these periods it became, I noticed, less and less easy to discover the house, to fit the key in the door, or, having gained access to the temple, to realise the visions

I *thought* I craved for.

Often, in this way, have I searched in vain for days, but only succeeded in losing myself in the murky purlieus of a quite strange Bloomsbury; stopping outside numberless counterfeit doors, and struggling vainly with locks that knew nothing of my little shining key.

But, on the other hand, pain, loneliness, sorrow – the merest whisper of spiritual affliction – and, lo, in a single moment the difficult geography became plain, and without hesitation, when I was unhappy or distressed, I found the way to his house as by a bird's instinctive flight, and the key slipped into the lock as though it loved it and was returning home.

The other cause to render him inaccessible, though not so determined – since it never concealed the way to the house – was even more distressing, for it depended wholly on myself; and I came to know how the least ugly action, involving a depreciation of ideals, so confused the mind that, when I got into the house, with difficulty, and found him in the little room after much searching, he was able to do or say scarcely anything at all for me. The mirror facing the door then gave back, I saw, no proper reflection of his person, but only a faded and wavering shadow with dim eyes and stooping, indistinct outline, and I even fancied I could see the pattern of the wall and shape of the furniture *through* his body, as though he had grown semi-transparent.

'You must not expect yearnings to weigh,' came his whisper, like wind far overhead, 'unless you lend to them *your own* substance; and your own substance you cannot both keep and lend. If you would know the Invisibles, forget yourself.'

And later, as the years slipped away one after another into the mists, and the frontier between the real and the unreal began to shift amazingly with his teachings, it became more and more clear to me that he belonged to a permanent region that, with all the changes in the world's history, has itself never altered in any essential particular. This immemorial Old Man of Visions, as I grew to think of him, had existed always; he was old as the sea and coeval with the stars; and he dwelt beyond time and space, reaching out a hand to all those who, weary of the shadows and illusions of practical life, really call to him with their heart of hearts. To me, indeed, the touch of sorrow was always near enough to prevent his becoming often inaccessible, and after a while even his voice became so *living* that I sometimes heard it calling to me in the street and in the fields.

Oh, wonderful Old Man of Visions! Happy the days of disaster, since they taught me how to know you, the Unraveller of Problems, the Destroyer of Doubts, who bore me ever away with soft flight down the long, long vistas of the heart and soul!

And his loneliness in that temple attic under the stars, his loneliness, too, had a meaning I did not fail to understand later, and why he was always available for me and seemed to belong to no other.

'To everyone who finds me,' he said, with the strange smile that wrapped his whole being and not his face alone, 'to every one I am the same, and yet different. I am not really ever alone. The whole world, nay' – his voice rose to a singing cry – 'the whole universe lies in this room, or just beyond that window-pane; for here past and future meet and all real dreams find completeness. But remember,' he added – and there was a sound as of soft wind and rain in the room with his voice – 'no true dream can ever be shared, and should you seek to explain me to another you must lose me beyond recall. You have never asked my name, nor must you ever tell it. Each must find me in his own way.'

Yet one day, for all my knowledge and his warnings, I felt so sure of my intimacy with this immemorial being, that I spoke of him to a friend who was, I had thought, so much a part of myself that it seemed no betrayal. And my friend, who went to search and found nothing, returned with the fool's laughter on his face, and swore that no street or number existed, for he had looked in vain, and had repeatedly *asked the way*.

And, from that day to this, the Old Man of Visions has neither called to me nor let his place be found; the streets are strange and empty, and I have even lost the little shining key.

The South Wind

IT IS IMPOSSIBLE to say through which sense or combination of senses, I knew that Someone was approaching – was already near; but most probably it was the deep underlying 'mother-sense' including them all that conveyed the delicate warning. At any rate, the scene-shifters of my moods knew it too, for very swiftly they prepared the stage; then, ever soft-footed and invisible, stood aside to wait.

As I went down the village street on my way to bed after midnight, the high Alpine valley lay silent in its frozen stillness. For days it had now lain thus, even the mouths of its cataracts stopped with ice; and for days, too, the dry, tight cold had drawn up the nerves of the humans in it to a sharp, thin pitch of exhilaration that at last began to call for the gentler comfort of relaxation. The key had been a little too high, the inner tautness too prolonged. The tension of that implacable north-east wind, the *bise noire*, had drawn its twisted wires too long through our very entrails. We all sighed for some loosening of the bands – the comforting touch of something damp, soft, less penetratingly acute.

And now, as I turned, midway in the little journey from the inn to my room above La Poste, this sudden warning that Someone was approaching repeated its silent wireless message, and I paused to listen and to watch.

Yet at first I searched in vain. The village street lay empty – a white ribbon between the black walls of the big-roofed chalets; there were no lights in any of the houses; the hotels stood gaunt and ugly with their myriad shuttered windows; and the church, topped by the Crown of Savoy in stone, was so engulfed by the shadows of the mountains that it seemed almost a part of them.

Beyond, reared the immense buttresses of the Dent du Midi, terrible and stalwart against the sky, their feet resting among the crowding pines, their streaked precipices tilting up at violent angles towards the stars. The bands of snow, belting their enormous flanks, stretched for miles, faintly gleaming, like Saturn's rings. To the right I could just make out the pinnacles of the Dents Blanches, cruelly pointed; and, still farther, the Dent de Bonnaveau, as of iron and crystal, running up its gaunt and dreadful pyramid into relentless depths of night. Everywhere in the hard, black-sparkling air was the rigid spell of winter. It seemed as if this valley could never melt again, never know currents of warm wind, never taste the sun, nor yield its million flowers.

And now, dipping down behind me out of the reaches of the darkness, the New Comer moved close, heralded by this subtle yet compelling admonition that had arrested me in my very tracks. For, just as I turned in at the door, kicking the crunched snow from my boots against the granite step, I *knew* that, from the heart of all this tightly frozen winter's night, the 'Someone' whose message had travelled so delicately in advance was now, quite suddenly, at my very heels. And while my eyes lifted to sift their way between the darkness and the snow I became aware that It was already coming down the village street. It ran on feathered feet, pressing close against the enclosing walls, yet at the same time spreading from side to side, brushing the window-panes, rustling against the doors, and even including the shingled roofs in its enveloping advent. It came, too – *against the wind*. . . .

It flew up close and passed me, very faintly singing, running down between the chalets and the church, very swift, very soft, neither man nor animal, neither woman, girl, nor child, turning the corner of the snowy road beyond the *Cure's* house with a rushing, cantering motion, that made me think of a Body of water – something of fluid and generous shape, too mighty to be confined in common forms. And, as it passed, it touched me – touched me through all skin and flesh upon the naked nerves, loosening, relieving, setting free the congealed sources of life which the *bise* so long had mercilessly bound, so that magic currents, flowing and released, washed down all the secret byways of the spirit and flooded again with full tide into a thousand dried-up cisterns of the heart.

The thrill I experienced is quiet incommunicable in words.

I ran upstairs and opened all my windows wide, knowing that soon the Messenger would return with a million others – only to find that already it had been there before me. Its taste was in the air, fragrant and alive; in my very mouth – and all the currents of the inner life ran sweet again, and full. Nothing in the whole village was quite the same as it had been before. The deeply slumbering peasants even, behind their shuttered windows and barred doors; the *Cure*, the servants at the inn, the consumptive man opposite, the children in the house behind the church, the horde of tourists in the caravanserai – all knew – more or less, according to the delicacy of their receiving apparatus – that Something charged with fresh and living force had swept on viewless feet down the village street, passed noiselessly between the cracks of doors and windows, touched nerves and eyelids, and – set them free. In response to the great Order of Release that the messenger had left everywhere behind her, even the dreams of the sleepers had shifted into softer and more flowing keys. . . .

And the Valley – the Valley also knew! For, as I watched from my window, something loosened about the trees and stones and boulders; about the massed snows on the great slopes; about the roots of the hanging icicles that fringed and sheeted the dark cliffs; and down in the deepest beds of the killed and silent streams. Far overhead, across those desolate bleak shoulders of the mountains, ran some sudden softness like the rush of awakening life . . . and was gone. A touch, lithe yet dewy, as of silk and water mixed, dropped softly over all . . . and, silently, without resistance, the *bise noire*, utterly routed, went back to the icy caverns of the north and east, where it sleeps, hated of men, and dreams its keen black dreams of death and desolation. . . .

. . . And some five hours later, when I woke and looked towards the sunrise, I saw those strips of pearly grey, just tinged with red, the Messenger had been to summon . . . charged with the warm moisture that brings relief. On the wings of a rising South Wind they came down hurriedly to cap the mountains and to unbind the captive forces of life; then moved with flying streamers up our own valley, sponging from the thirsty woods their richest perfume. . . .

And farther down, in soft, wet fields, stood the leafless poplars, with little pools of water gemming the grass between and pouring their musical overflow through runnels of dark and sodden leaves to join the rapidly increasing torrents descending from the mountains. For across the entire valley ran magically that sweet and welcome message of relief which Job knew when he put the whole delicious tenderness and passion of it into less than a dozen words: '*He comforteth the earth with the south wind.*'

CHAMPERY.

The Touch of Pan

I

AN IDIOT, Heber understood, was a person in whom intelligence had been arrested – instinct acted, but not reason. A lunatic, on the other hand, was someone whose reason had gone awry – the mechanism of the brain was injured. The lunatic was out of relation with his environment; the idiot had merely been delayed *en route*.

Be that as it might, he knew at any rate that a lunatic was not to be listened to, whereas an idiot – well, the one he fell in love with certainly had the secret of some instinctual knowledge that was not only joy, but a kind of sheer natural joy. Probably it was that sheer natural joy of living that reason argues to be untaught, degraded. In any case – at thirty – he married her instead of the daughter of a duchess he was engaged to. They lead today that happy, natural, vagabond life called idiotic, unmindful of that world the majority of reasonable people live only to remember.

Though born into an artificial social clique that made it difficult, Heber had always loved the simple things. Nature, especially, meant much to him. He would rather see a woodland misty with bluebells than all the chateaux on the Loire; the thought of a mountain valley in the dawn made his feet lonely in the grandest houses. Yet in these very houses was his home established. Not that he underestimated worldly things – their value was too obvious – but that it was another thing he wanted. Only he did not know precisely *what* he wanted until this particular idiot made it plain.

Her case was a mild one, possibly; the title bestowed by implication rather than by specific mention. Her family did not say that she was imbecile or half-witted, but that she was 'not all there' they probably did say. Perhaps she saw men as trees walking, perhaps she saw through a glass darkly. . . .

84

Heber, who had met her once or twice, though never yet to speak to, did not analyse her degree of sight, for in him, personally, she woke a secret joy and wonder that almost involved a touch of awe. The part of her that was 'not all there' dwelt in an 'elsewhere' that he longed to know about. He wanted to share it with her. She seemed aware of certain happy and desirable things that reason and too much thinking hid.

He just felt this instinctively without analysis. The values they set upon the prizes of life were similar. Money to her was just stamped metal, fame a loud noise of sorts, position nothing. Of people she was aware as a dog or bird might be aware — they were kind or unkind. Her parents, having collected much metal and achieved position, proceeded to make a loud noise of sorts with some success; and since she did not contribute, either by her appearance or her tastes, to their ambitions, they neglected her and made excuses. They were ashamed of her existence. Her father in particular justified Nietzsche's shrewd remark that no one with a loud voice can listen to subtle thoughts.

She was, perhaps, sixteen; for, though she did not look it, eighteen or nineteen was probably more in accord with her birth certificate. Her mother was content, however, that she should dress the lesser age, preferring to tell strangers that she was childish, rather than admit that she was backward.

'You'll never marry at all, child, much less marry as you might,' she said, 'if you go about with that rabbit expression on your face. That's not the way to catch a nice young man of the sort we get down to stay with us now. Many a chorus-girl with less than you've got has caught them easily enough. Your sister's done well. Why not do the same? There's nothing to be shy or frightened about.'

'But I'm not shy or frightened, mother. I'm bored. I mean *they* bore me.'

It made no difference to the girl; she was herself. The bored expression in the eyes — the rabbit, not-all-there expression — gave place sometimes to another look. Yet not often, nor with anybody. It was this other look that stirred the strange joy in the man who fell in love with her. It is not to be easily described. It was very wonderful. Whether sixteen or nineteen, she then looked – a thousand.

*　　　*　　　*

The house-party was of that up-to-date kind prevalent in Heber's world. Husbands and wives were not asked together. There was a cynical disregard of the decent (not the stupid) conventions that savoured of abandon, perhaps of decadence. He only went himself in the hope of seeing the backward daughter once again. Her millionaire parents afflicted him, the smart folk tired him. Their peculiar affectation of a special language, their strange belief that they were of importance, their treatment of the servants, their calculated self-indulgence, all jarred upon him more than usual. At bottom he heartily despised the whole vapid set. He felt uncomfortable and out of place. Though not a prig, he abhorred the way these folk believed themselves the climax of fine living. Their open immorality disgusted him, their indiscriminate love-making was merely rather nasty; he watched the very girl he was at last to settle down with behaving as the tone of the clique expected over her final fling – and, bored by the strain of so much 'modernity', he tried to get away. Tea was long over, the sunset interval invited, he felt hungry for trees and fields that were not self-conscious – and he escaped. The flaming June day was turning chilly. Dusk hovered over the ancient house, veiling the pretentious new wing that had been added. And he came across the idiot girl at the bend of the drive, where the birch trees shivered in the evening wind. His heart gave a sudden leap.

She was leaning against one of the dreadful statues – it was a satyr – that sprinkled the lawn. Her back was to him; she gazed at a group of broken pine trees in the park beyond. He paused an instant, then went on quickly, while his mind scurried to recall her name. They were within easy speaking range.

'Miss Elizabeth!' he cried, yet not too loudly, lest she might vanish as suddenly as she had appeared. She turned at once. Her eyes and lips were smiling welcome at him without pretence. She showed no surprise.

'You're the first one of the lot who's said it properly,' she exclaimed, as he came up. 'Everybody calls me Elizabeth instead of Elspeth. It's idiotic. They don't even take the trouble to get a name right.'

'It is,' he agreed, 'quite idiotic.' He did not correct her. Possibly he had said Elspeth after all – the names were similar. Her perfectly natural voice was grateful to his ear, and soothing. He looked at her all over with an open admiration that she noticed and, without concealment, liked. She was very untidy, the grey stockings on her slim, vigorous legs were torn, her short skirt was spattered with mud. Her nut-brown hair, glossy and plentiful, flew loose about neck and shoulders. In place of the usual belt she had tied a coloured handkerchief round her waist. She wore no hat. What she had been doing to get in such a state, while her parents entertained a 'distinguished' party, he did not know, but it was not difficult to guess. Climbing trees or riding bareback and astride was probably the truth. Yet her dishevelled state became her well, and the welcome in her face delighted him. She remembered him, she was glad. He, too, was glad, and a sense both happy and reckless stirred in his heart. 'Like a wild animal,' he said, 'you come out in the dusk —'

'To play with my kind,' she answered in a flash, throwing him a glance of invitation that made his blood go dancing.

He leaned against the statue a moment, asking himself why this young Cinderella of a parvenu family delighted him when all the London beauties left him cold. There was a lift through his whole being as he watched her, slim and supple, grace shining through the untidy modern garb – almost as though she wore no clothes. He thought of a panther standing upright. Her poise was so alert – one arm upon the marble ledge, one leg bent across the other, the hip-line showing like a bird's curved wing. Wild animal or bird, flashed across his mind; something untamed and natural. Another second and she might leap away – or spring into his arms.

It was a deep, delicious sensation in him that produced the mental picture. 'Pure and natural,' a voice whispered with it in his heart, 'as surely as *they* are just the other thing!' And the thrill struck with unerring aim at the very root of that unrest he had always known in the state of life to which he was called. She made the natural clean and pure. This girl and himself were somehow kin. The primitive thing broke loose in him.

In two seconds, while he stood with her beside the vulgar statue, these thoughts passed through his mind. But he did not at first give utterance to any of them. He spoke more formally, although laughter, due to his happiness, lay close behind.

'They haven't asked you to the party, then? Or you don't care about it? Which is it?'

'Both,' she said, looking fearlessly into his face. 'But I've been waiting here ten minutes already. Why were you so long?'

This outspoken honesty was hardly what he expected, yet in another sense he was not surprised. Her eyes were very penetrating, very innocent, very frank. He felt her as clean and sweet as some young fawn that asks plainly to be stroked and fondled. He told the truth: 'I couldn't get away before. I had to play about and —' when she interrupted with impatience:

'*They* don't want you,' she exclaimed scornfully. 'I do.'

And, before he could choose one out of the several answers that rushed into his mind, she nudged him with her foot, holding it out a little so that he saw the shoelace was unfastened. She nodded her head towards it, and pulled her skirt up half an inch as he at once stooped down.

'And, anyhow,' she went on as he fumbled with the lace, touching her ankle with his hand, 'you're going to marry one of them. I read it in the paper. You'll be miserable. It's idiotic.'

The blood rushed to his head, but whether owing to his stooping or to something else, he could not say.

'I only came – I only accepted,' he said quickly, 'because I wanted to see you again.'

'Of course. I made mother ask you.'

He did an impulsive thing. Kneeling as he was, he bent his head a little lower and suddenly kissed the soft grey stocking – then stood up and looked her in the face. She was

88

laughing happily, no sign of embarrassment in her anywhere, no trace of outraged modesty. She only looked very pleased.

'I've tied a knot that won't come undone in a hurry —' he began, then stopped dead. For as he said it, gazing into her smiling face, another expression looked forth at him from the two big eyes of hazel. Something rushed from his heart to meet it. It may have been that playful kiss, it may have been the way she took it; but, at any rate, there was a strength in the new emotion that made him unsure of who he was and of whom he looked at. He forgot the place, the time, his own identity and hers. ... The lawn swept from beneath his feet, the English sunset with it. He forgot his host and hostess, his fellow guests, even his father's name and his own into the bargain. He was carried away upon a great tide, the girl always beside him. He left the shore-line in the distance, already half forgotten, the shore-line of his education, learning, manners, social point of view – everything to which his father had most carefully brought him up as the scion of an old-established English family. This girl had torn up the anchor. Only the anchor had previously been loosened a little, perhaps, by his own unconscious and restless efforts. ...

Where was she taking him to? Upon what island would they land ... ?

'I'm younger than you – a good deal,' she broke in upon his rushing mood. 'But that doesn't matter a bit, does it? We're about the same age really.'

With the happy sound of her voice the extraordinary sensation passed – or, rather, it became normal. But that it lasted an appreciable time was proved by the fact that they had left the statue on the lawn, the house was no longer visible behind them, and they were now walking side by side between the massive rhododendron clumps. They brought up against a five-barred gate into the park. They leaned upon the topmost bar, and he felt her shoulder touching his – edging into it – as they looked across to the grove of pines.

'I feel absurdly young,' he said without a sign of affectation, 'and yet I've been looking for you a thousand years and more.'

The afterglow lit up her face; it fell on her loose hair and tumbled blouse, turning them amber red. She looked not only soft and comely, but extraordinarily beautiful. The strange expression haunted the deep eyes again, the lips were a little parted, the young breast heaving slightly, joy and excitement in her whole presentment. And as he watched her he knew that all he had just felt was due to her close presence, her atmosphere, her perfume, her physical warmth and vigour. It had emanated directly from her being.

'Of course,' she said, and laughed so that he felt her breath upon his face. He bent lower to bring his own on a level, gazing straight into her eyes that were still fixed upon the field beyond. They were clear and luminous as pools of water, and in their centre, sharp as a photograph, he saw the reflection of the pine grove, perhaps a hundred yards away. With detailed accuracy he saw it, empty and motionless in the glimmering June dusk.

Then something caught his eye. He examined the picture more closely. He drew slightly nearer. He almost touched her face with his own, forgetting for a moment whose were the eyes that served him for a mirror. For, looking intently thus, it seemed to him that there was movement, a passing to and fro, a stirring as of figures among the trees. . . . Then suddenly the entire picture was obliterated. She had dropped her lids. He heard her speaking – the warm breath was again upon his face:

'*In the heart of that wood dwell I.*'

His heart gave another leap – more violent than the first – for the sentence caught him like a spell. There was a lilt and rhythm in the words, a wonder and a beauty, that made it poetry. She laid emphasis upon the pronoun and the nouns. It seemed the last line of some delicious runic verse:

'In the *heart* of that *wood* – dwell *I*. . . .'

And it flashed across him: That living, moving, inhabited pine wood was her thought. It was thus she thought it, saw it. Her nature flung back to a life she understood, a life that needed, claimed her. The ostentatious and artificial values that surrounded her she denied, even as the distinguished house-party of her ambitious, masquerading family neglected her. Of course she was unnoticed by them – just as a swallow or a wild-rose were unnoticed.

He knew her secret then, for she had told it to him. It was his own secret too. They were akin, as the birds and animals were akin. They belonged together in some free and open life, natural, wild, untamed. That unhampered life was flowing about them now, rising, beating with delicious tumult in her veins and his, yet innocent as the sunlight and the wind – because it was as freely recognised.

'Elspeth!' he cried, 'come, take me with you! We'll go at once. Come – hurry – before we forget to be happy, or remember to be wise again —!'

His words stopped half-way towards completion, for a perfume floated past him, born of the summer dusk, perhaps, yet sweet with a penetrating magic that made his senses reel with some remembered joy. No flower, no scented garden-bush delivered it. It was the perfume of young, spendthrift life, sweet with the purity that reason had not yet stained. The girl moved closer. Gathering her loose hair between her fingers, she brushed his cheeks and eyes with it, her slim, warm body pressing against him as she leaned over laughingly.

'In the darkness,' she whispered in his ear; 'when the moon puts the house upon the statue!'

And he understood. Her world lay behind the vulgar, staring day. He turned. He heard the flutter of skirts – just caught the grey stockings, swift and light, as they flew behind the rhododendron masses. And she was gone.

He stood a long time, leaning upon that five-barred gate. . . . It was the dressing-gong that recalled him at length to what seemed the present. By the conservatory door, as he went slowly in, he met his distinguished cousin – who was helping the girl he himself was to marry to enjoy her 'final fling.' He looked at his cousin. He realised suddenly that he was merely vicious. There was no sun and wind, no flowers – there was depravity only, lust instead of laughter, excitement in place of happiness. It was calculated, not spontaneous. His mind was in it. Without joy it was. He was not natural.

'Not a girl in the whole lot fit to look at,' his cousin exclaimed with peevish boredom, excusing himself stupidly for his illicit conduct. 'I'm off in the morning.' He shrugged his blue-blooded shoulders. 'These millionaires! Their shooting's all right, but their mixum-gatherum week-ends – bah!' His gesture completed all he had to say about this one in particular. He glanced sharply, nastily, at his companion. '*You* look as if you'd found something!' he added, with a suggestive grin. 'Or have you seen the ghost that was paid for with the house?' And he guffawed and let his eye-glass drop. 'Lady Hermione will be asking for an explanation – eh?'

'Idiot!' replied Heber, and ran upstairs to dress for dinner.

But the word was wrong, he remembered, as he closed his door. It was lunatic he had meant to say, yet something more as well. He saw the smart, modern philanderer somehow as a beast.

2

IT WAS nearly midnight when he went up to bed, after an evening of intolerable amusement. The abandoned moral attitude, the common rudeness, the contempt of all others but themselves, the ugly jests, the horseplay of tasteless minds that passed for gaiety, above all the shamelessness of the women that behind the cover of fine breeding aped emancipation, afflicted him to a boredom that touched desperation.

He understood now with a clarity unknown before. As with his cousin, so with these. They took life, he saw, with a brazen effrontery they thought was freedom, while yet it was life that they denied. He felt vampired and degraded; spontaneity went out of him. The fact that the geography of bedrooms was studied openly seemed an affirmation of vice that sickened him. Their ways were nauseous merely. He escaped – unnoticed.

He locked his door, went to the open window, and looked out into the night – then started. For silver dressed the lawn and park, the shadow of the building lay dark across the elaborate garden, and the moon, he noticed, was just high enough to put the house upon the statue. The chimney-stacks edged the pedestal precisely.

'Odd!' he exclaimed. 'Odd that I should come at the very moment —!' then smiled as he realised how his proposed adventure would be misinterpreted, its natural innocence and spirit ruined – if he were seen. 'And someone would be sure to see me on a night like this. There are couples still hanging about in the garden.' And he glanced at the shrubberies and secret paths that seemed to float upon the warm June air like islands.

He stood for a moment framed in the glare of the electric light, then turned back into the room; and at that instant a low sound like a bird-call rose from the lawn below. It was soft and flutey, as though someone played two notes upon a reed, a piping sound. He had been seen, and she was waiting for him. Before he knew it, he had made an answering call, of oddly similar kind, then switched the light out.

Three minutes later, dressed in simpler clothes, with a cap pulled over his eyes, he reached the back lawn by means of the conservatory and billiard-room. He paused a moment to look about him. There was no one, although the lights were still ablaze. 'I am an idiot,' he chuckled to himself. 'I'm acting on instinct!' He ran.

The sweet night air bathed him from head to foot; there was strength and cleansing in it. The lawn shone wet with dew. He could almost smell the perfume of the stars. The fumes of wine, cigars, and artificial scent were left behind, the atmosphere exhaled by civilisation, by heavy thoughts, by bodies overdressed, unwisely stimulated – all, all forgotten. He passed into a world of magical enchantment. The hush of the open sky came down. In black and white the garden lay, brimmed full with beauty, shot by the ancient silver of the moon, spangled with the stars' old-gold. And the night wind rustled in the rhododendron masses as he flew between them.

In a moment he was beside the statue, engulfed now by the shadow of the building, and the girl detached herself silently from the blur of darkness. Two arms were flung about his neck, a shower of soft hair fell on his cheek with a heady scent of earth and leaves and grass, and the same instant they were away together at full speed – towards the pine wood. Their feet were soundless on the soaking grass. They went so swiftly that they made a whir of following wind that blew her hair across his eyes.

And the sudden contrast caused a shock that put a blank, perhaps, upon his mind, so that he lost the standard of remembered things. For it was no longer merely a particular adventure; it seemed a habit and a natural joy resumed.

It was not new. He realised the momentum of an accustomed happiness, mislaid, it may be, but certainly familiar. They sped across the gravel paths that intersected the well-groomed lawn, they leaped the flower-beds, so laboriously shaped in mockery, they clambered over the ornamental iron railings, scorning the easier five-barred gate into the park. The longer grass then shook the dew in soaking showers against his knees. He stooped, as though in some foolish effort to turn up something, then realised that his legs, of course, were bare. *Her* garment was already high and free, for she, too, was barelegged like himself. He saw her little ankles, wet and shining in the moonlight, and flinging himself down, he kissed them happily, plunging his face into the dripping, perfumed grass. Her ringing laughter mingled with his own, as she stooped beside him the same instant; her hair hung in a silver cloud; her eyes gleamed through its curtain into his; then, suddenly, she soaked her hands in the heavy dew and passed them over his face with a softness that was like the touch of some scented southern wind.

'Now you are anointed with the Night,' she cried. 'No one will know you. You are forgotten of the world. Kiss me!'

'We'll play for ever and ever,' he cried, 'the eternal game that was old when still the world was young,' and lifting her in his arms he kissed her eyes and lips. There was some natural bliss of song and dance and laughter in his heart, an elemental bliss that caught them together as wind and sunlight catch the branches of a tree. She leaped from the ground to meet his swinging arms, and in an instant was upon his shoulders. He ran with her, then tossed her off and caught her neatly as she fell. Evading a second capture, she danced ahead, holding out one shining arm that he might

94

follow. Hand in hand they raced on together through the clean summer moonlight. Yet there remained a smooth softness as of fur against his neck and shoulders, and he saw then that she wore skins of tawny colour that clung to her body closely, that he wore them too, and that her skin, like his own, was of a sweet dusky brown.

Then, pulling her towards him, he stared into her face. She suffered the close gaze a second, but no longer, for with a burst of sparkling laughter again she leaped into his arms, and before he shook her free she had pulled and tweaked the two small horns that hid in the thick curly hair behind, and just above, the ears.

And that wilful tweaking turned him wild and reckless. That touch ran down him deep into the mothering earth. He leaped and ran and sang with a great laughing sound. The wine of eternal youth flushed all his veins with joy, and the old, old world was young again with every impulse of natural happiness intensified with the Earth's own foaming tide of life.

From head to foot he tingled with the delight of Spring, prodigal with creative power. Of course he could fly the bushes and fling wild across the open! Of course the wind and moonlight fitted close and soft about him like a skin! Of course he had youth and beauty for playmates, with dancing, laughter, singing, and a thousand kisses! For he and she were natural once again. They were free together of those long-forgotten days when 'Pan leaped through the roses in the month of June . . . !'

With the girl swaying this way and that upon his shoulders, tweaking his horns with mischief and desire, hanging her flying hair before his eyes, then bending swiftly over again to lift it, he danced to join the rest of their companions in the little moonlit grove of pines beyond. . . .

3

THEY ROSE somewhat pointed, perhaps, against the moonlight, those English pines – more with the shape of cypresses, some might have thought. A stream gushed down between their roots, there were mossy ferns, and rough grey boulders with lichen on them. But there was no dimness, for the silver of the moon sprinkled freely through the branches like the faint sunlight that it really was, and the air ran out to meet them with a heady fragrance that was wiser far than wine.

The girl, in an instant, was whirled from her perch on his shoulders and caught by a dozen arms that bore her into the heart of the merry, careless throng. Whisht! Whew! Whir! She was gone, but another, fairer still, was in her place, with skins as soft and knees that clung as tightly. Her eyes were liquid amber, grapes hung between her little breasts, her arms entwined about him, smoother than marble, and as cool. She had a crystal laugh.

But he flung her off, so that she fell plump among a group of bigger figures lolling against a twisted root and roaring with a jollity that boomed like wind through the chorus of a song. They seized her, kissed her, then sent her flying. They were happier, after all, with their glad singing. They held stone goblets, red and foaming in their broad-palmed hands.

'The mountains lie behind us!' cried someone dancing past. 'We are come at last into our valley of delight. Grapes, breasts, and rich red lips! Ho! Ho! It is time to press them that the juice of life may run!' The figure waved a cluster of ferns across the air and vanished amid a cloud of song and laughter.

'It is ours. Use it!' answered a deep, ringing voice. 'The valleys are our own. No climbing now!' And a wind of echoing cries gave answer from all sides. 'Life! Life! Life! Abundant, flowing over – use it, use it!'

A troop of nymphs rushed forth, escaped from clustering arms and lips they yet openly desired. He chased them in and out among the waving branches, while she who had brought him ever followed, and sped past him and away again. He caught three gleaming soft brown bodies, then fell beneath them, smothered, bubbling with joyous laughter – next freed himself and, while they sought to drag him captive again, escaped and raced with a leap upon a slimmer, sweeter outline that swung up – only just in time – upon a lower bough, whence she leaned down above him with hanging net of hair and merry eyes. A few feet beyond his reach, she laughed and teased him – the one who had brought him in, the one he ever sought, and who for ever sought him too. ....

It became a riotous glory of wild children who romped and played with an impassioned glee beneath the moon. For the world was young and they, her happy offspring, glowed with the life she poured so freely into them. All intermingled, the laughing voices rose into a foam of song that broke against the stars. The difficult mountains had been climbed and were forgotten. Good! Then, enjoy the luxuriant, fruitful valley and be glad! And glad they were, brimful with spontaneous energy, natural as birds and animals that obeyed the big, deep rhythm of a simpler age — natural as wind and innocent as sunshine.

Yet, for all the untamed riot, there was a lift of beauty pulsing underneath. Even when the wildest abandon approached the heat of orgy, when the recklessness appeared excess — there hid that marvellous touch of loveliness which makes the natural sacred. There was coherence, purpose, the fulfilling of an exquisite law: and — there was worship. The form it took, haply, was strange as well as riotous, yet in its strangeness dreamed innocence and purity, and in its very riot flamed that spirit which is divine.

For he found himself at length beside her once again; breathless and panting, her sweet brown limbs aglow from the excitement of escape denied; eyes shining like a blaze of stars, and pulses beating with tumultuous life — helpless and yielding against the strength that pinned her down between the roots. His eyes put mastery on her own. She looked up into his face, obedient, happy, soft with love, surrendering with the same delicious abandon that had swept her for a moment into other arms. 'You caught me in the end,' she sighed. 'I only played awhile.'

'I hold you for ever,' he replied, half wondering at the rough power in his voice.

It was here the hush of worship stole upon her little face, into her obedient eyes, about her parted lips. She ceased her wilful struggling.

'Listen!' she whispered. 'I hear a step upon the glades beyond. The iris and the lily open; the earth is ready, waiting; we must be ready too! *He* is coming!'

He released her and sprang up; the entire company rose

too. All stood, all bowed the head. There was an instant's subtle panic, but it was the panic of reverent awe that preludes a descent of deity. For a wind passed through the branches with a sound that is the oldest in the world and so the youngest. Above it there rose the shrill, faint piping of a little reed. ...

Only the first, true sounds were audible – wind and water: the tinkling of the dewdrops as they fell, the murmur of the trees against the air. This was the piping that they heard. And in the hush the stars bent down to hear, the riot paused, the orgy passed and died. The figures waited, kneeling then with one accord. They listened with – the Earth.

'He comes. ... He comes ...' the valley breathed about them.

A footfall from far away came treading across a world unruined and unstained. It fell with the wind and water, sweetening the valley into life as it approached. Across the rivers and forests it came gently, tenderly, but swiftly and with a power that knew majesty.

'He comes. ... He comes ... !' rose with the murmur of the wind and water from the host of lowered heads.

The footfall came nearer, treading a world grown soft with worship. It reached the grove. It entered. There was a sense of intolerable loveliness, of brimming life, of rapture. The thousand faces lifted like a cloud. They heard the piping close. ... And so He came.

But He came with blessing. With the stupendous Presence there was joy, the joy of abundant, natural life, pure as the sunlight and the wind. He passed among them. There was great movement – as of a forest shaking, as of deep water falling, as of a cornfield swaying to the wind, gentle as of a harebell shedding its burden of dew that it has held too long because of love. He passed among them, touching every head. The great hand swept with tenderness each face, lingered a moment on each beating heart. There was sweetness, peace, and loveliness; but above all, there was – life. He sanctioned every natural joy in them and blessed each passion with his power of creation. ... Yet each one saw him differently: some as a wife or maiden desired with fire, some as a youth or stalwart husband, others as a figure veiled with stars or cloaked in luminous mist, hardly attainable; others, again – the fewest these, not more than two or three – as that mysterious wonder which tempts the heart away from known familiar sweetness into a wilderness of undecipherable magic without flesh and blood.

To two, in particular, He came so near that they could feel his breath of hills and fields upon their eyes. He touched them with both mighty hands. He stroked the marble breasts, He felt the little hidden horns ... and, as they bent lower so that their lips met together for an instant, He took her arms and twined them about the curved, brown neck that she might hold him closer still. ...

Again a footfall sounded far away upon an unruined world ... and He was gone – back into the wind and water whence He came. The thousand faces lifted; all stood up; the hush of worship still among them. There was a quiet as of the dawn. The piping floated over woods and fields, fading into silence. All looked at one another. ... And then once more the laughter and the play broke loose.

4

'WE'LL GO,' she cried, 'and peep upon that other world where life hangs like a prison on their eyes!'

And, in a moment, they were across the soaking grass, the lawn and flower-beds, and close to the walls of the heavy mansion. He peered in through a window, lifting her up to peer in with him. He recognised the world to which he outwardly belonged; he understood; a little gasp escaped him; and a slight shiver ran down the girl's body into his own. She turned her eyes away. 'See,' she murmured in his ear, 'it's ugly, it's not natural. They feel guilty and ashamed. There is no innocence!' She saw the men; it was the women that he saw chiefly.

Lolling ungracefully, with a kind of boldness that asserted independence, the women smoked their cigarettes with an air of invitation they sought to conceal and yet plainly showed. He saw his familiar world in nakedness. Their backs were bare, for all the elaborate clothes they wore; they hung their breasts uncleanly; in their eyes shone light that had never known the open sun. Hoping they were alluring and desirable, they feigned a guilty ignorance of that hope. They all pretended. Instead of wind and dew upon their hair, he saw flowers grown artificially to ape wild beauty, tresses without lustre borrowed from the slums of city factories. He watched the manoeuvring with the men; heard dark sentences; caught gestures half delivered whose meaning should just convey that glimpse of guilt they deemed to increase pleasure. The women were calculating, but nowhere glad; the men experienced, but nowhere joyous. Pretended innocence lay cloaked with a veil of something that whispered secretly, clandestine, ashamed, yet with a brazen air that laid mockery instead of sunshine in their smiles. Vice masqueraded in the ugly shape of pleasure; beauty was degraded into calculated tricks. They were not natural. They knew not joy.

'The forward ones, the civilised!' she laughed in his ear, tweaking his horns with energy. '*We* are the backward!'

'Unclean,' he muttered, recalling a catchword of the world he gazed upon.

They were the civilised! They were refined and educated – advanced. Generations of careful breeding, mate cautiously selecting mate, laid the polish of caste upon their hands and faces where gleamed ridiculous, untaught jewels – rings, bracelets, necklaces hanging absurdly from every possible angle.

'But – they are dressed up – for fun,' he exclaimed, more to himself than to the girl in skins who clung to his shoulder with her naked arms.

'*Un*dressed!' she answered, putting her brown hand in play across his eyes. 'Only they have forgotten even that!' And another shiver passed through her into him. He turned and hid his face against the soft skins that touched his cheek. He kissed her body. Seizing his horns, she pressed him to her, laughing happily.

'Look!' she whispered, raising her head again; 'they're coming out.' And he saw that two of them, a man and a girl, with an interchange of secret glances, had stolen from the room and were already by the door of the conservatory that led into the garden. It was his wife to be – and his distinguished cousin.

'Oh, Pan!' she cried in mischief. The girl sprang from his arms and pointed. 'We will follow them. We will put natural life into their little veins!'

'Or panic terror,' he answered, catching the yellow panther skin and following her swiftly round the building. He kept in the shadow, though she ran full into the blaze of moonlight. 'But they can't see us,' she called, looking over her shoulder a moment. 'They can only feel our presence, perhaps.' And, as she danced across the lawn, it seemed a moonbeam slipped from a sapling birch tree that the wind curved earthwards, then tossed back against the sky.

Keeping just ahead, they led the pair, by methods known instinctively to elemental blood yet not translatable – led them towards the little grove of waiting pines. The night wind murmured in the branches; a bird woke into a sudden burst of song. These sounds were plainly audible. But four little pointed ears caught other, wilder, notes behind the wind and music of the bird – the cries and ringing laughter, the leaping footsteps and the happy singing of their merry kin within the wood.

And the throng paused then amid the revels to watch the 'civilised' draw near. They presently reached the trees, halted, looked about them, hesitated a moment – then, with a hurried movement as of shame and fear lest they be caught, entered the zone of shadow.

'Let's go in here,' said the man, without music in his voice. 'It's dry on the pine needles, and we can't be seen.' He led the way; she picked up her skirts and followed over the strip of long wet grass. 'Here's a log all ready for us,' he added, sat down, and drew her into his arms with a sigh of satisfaction. 'Sit on my knee; it's warmer for your pretty figure.' He chuckled; evidently they were on familiar terms, for though she hesitated there was no real resistance in her, and she allowed the ungraceful roughness. 'But are we *quite* safe? Are you sure?' she asked between his kisses.

'What does it matter, even if we're not?' he replied, establishing her more securely on his knees. 'But, as a matter of fact, we're safer here than in my own house.' He kissed her hungrily. 'By Jove, Hermione, but you're divine,' he cried passionately, 'divinely beautiful. I love you with every atom of my being – with my very soul.'

'Yes, dear, I know – I mean, I know you do, but —'

'But what?' he asked impatiently.

'Those horrid detectives —'

He laughed. Yet it seemed to annoy him. 'My wife *is* a beast, isn't she? – to have me watched like that,' he said quickly.

'They're everywhere,' she replied, a sudden hush in her tone. She looked at the encircling trees a moment, then added bitterly: 'I hate her, simply *hate* her for it.'

'I love you,' he cried, crushing her to him, 'that's all that matters now. Don't let's waste time talking about the rest.' She contrived to shudder, and hid her face against his coat, while he showered kisses on her neck and hair.

And the solemn pine trees watched them, the silvery moonlight fell on their faces, the scent of new-mown hay went floating past.

'I love you with my very soul,' he repeated with intense conviction. 'I'd do anything, give up anything, bear anything – just to give you a moment's happiness. I swear it – before God!'

There was a faint sound among the trees behind them, and the girl sat up, alert. She would have scrambled to her feet, but that he held her tight.

'What the devil's the matter with you tonight?' he asked in a different tone, his vexation plainly audible. 'You're as nervy as if *you* were being watched, instead of me.'

She paused before she answered, her finger on her lip. Then she spoke slowly, hushing her voice a little:

'Watched!' she repeated. 'That's exactly what I did feel. I've felt it ever since we came into the wood.'

'Nonsense, Hermione. It's too many cigarettes.' He drew her back into his arms, forcing her head up so that he could kiss her better.

'I suppose it is nonsense,' she said, smiling. 'It's gone now, anyhow.'

He began admiring her hair, her dress, her shoes, her pretty ankles, while she resisted in a way that proved her practice. 'It's not *me* you love,' she pouted, yet drinking in his praise. She listened to his repeated assurances that he loved her with his 'soul' and was prepared for any sacrifice.

'I feel so safe with you,' she murmured, knowing the moves in the game as well as he did. She looked up guiltily into his face, while he looked down with a passion that he thought perhaps was joy.

'You'll be married before the summer's out,' he said, 'and all the thrill and excitement will be over. Poor Hermione!' She lay back in his arms, drawing his face down with both hands, and kissing him on the lips. 'You'll have more of him than you can do with – eh? As much as you care about, anyhow.'

'I shall be much more free,' she whispered. 'Things will be easier. And I've got to marry someone —'

She broke off with another start. There was a sound again behind them. The man heard nothing. The blood in his temples pulsed too loudly, doubtless.

'Well, what is it this time?' he asked sharply.

She was peering into the wood, where the patches of dark shadow and moonlit spaces made odd, irregular patterns in the air. A low branch near them waved slightly in the wind.

'Did you hear?' she asked nervously.

'Wind,' he replied, annoyed that her change of mood disturbed his pleasure.

'But something moved —'

'Only a branch. We're quite alone, quite safe, I tell you,' and there was a rasping sound in his voice as he said it. 'Don't be so imaginative. I can take care of you.'

She sprang up. The moonlight caught her figure, revealing its exquisite young curves beneath the smother of the costly clothing. Her hair had dropped a little in the struggle. The man eyed her eagerly, making a quick, impatient gesture towards her, then stopped abruptly. He saw the terror in her eyes.

'Oh, hark! What's that?' she whispered in a startled voice. She put her finger up. 'Oh, let's go back. I don't like this wood. I'm frightened.'

'Rubbish,' he said, and tried to catch her by the waist.

'It's safer in the house – my room – or yours —' She broke off again. 'There it is – don't you hear? It's a footstep!' Her face was whiter than the moon.

'I tell you it's the wind in the branches,' he repeated gruffly. 'Oh, come on, *do*. We were just getting jolly together. There's nothing to be afraid of. Can't you believe me?' He tried to pull her down upon his knee again with force. His face wore an unpleasant expression that was half leer, half grin.

But the girl stood away from him. She continued to peer nervously about her. She listened intently.

'You give me the creeps,' he exclaimed crossly, clawing at her waist again with passionate eagerness that now betrayed exasperation. His disappointment turned him coarse.

The girl made a quick movement of escape, turning so as to look in every direction. She gave a little scream.

'That *was* a step. Oh, oh, it's close behind us. I heard it. We're being watched!' she cried in terror. She darted towards him, then shrank back. He did not try to touch her this time.

'Moonshine!' he growled. 'You've spoilt my — spoilt our chance with your silly nerves.'

But she did not hear him apparently. She stood there shivering as with sudden cold.

'There! I saw it again. I'm sure of it. Something went past me through the air.'

And the man, still thinking only of his own pleasure frustrated, got up heavily, something like anger in his eyes. 'All right,' he said testily; 'if you're going to make a fuss, we'd better go. The house *is* safer, possibly, as you say. You know my room. Come along!' Even that risk he would not take. He loved her with his 'soul.'

They crept stealthily out of the wood, the girl slightly in front of him, casting frightened backward glances. Afraid, guilty, ashamed, with an air as though they had been detected, they stole back towards the garden and the house, and disappeared from view.

And a wind rose suddenly with a rushing sound, poured through the wood as though to cleanse it, swept out the artificial scent and trace of shame, and brought back again the song, the laughter, and the happy revels. It roared across the park, it shook the windows of the house, then sank away as quickly as it came. The trees stood motionless again, guarding their secret in the clean, sweet moonlight that held the world in dream until the dawn stole up, and sunshine took the earth again with joy.

The Valley of the Beasts

I

As they emerged suddenly from the dense forest the Indian halted, and Grimwood, his employer, stood beside him, gazing into the beautiful wooded valley that lay spread below them in the blaze of a golden sunset. Both men leaned upon their rifles, caught by the enchantment of the unexpected scene.

'We camp here,' said Tooshalli abruptly, after a careful survey. 'Tomorrow we make a plan.'

He spoke excellent English. The note of decision, almost of authority, in his voice was noticeable, but Grimwood set it down to the natural excitement of the moment. Every track they had followed during the last two days, but one track in particular as well, had headed straight for this remote and hidden valley, and the sport promised to be unusual.

'That's so,' he replied, in the tone of one giving an order. 'You can make camp ready at once.' And he sat down on a fallen hemlock to take off his moccasin boots and grease his feet that ached from the arduous day now drawing to a close. Though under ordinary circumstances he would have pushed on for another hour or two, he was not averse to a night here, for exhaustion had come upon him during the last bit of rough going, his eye and muscles were no longer steady, and it was doubtful if he could have shot straight enough to kill. He did not mean to miss a second time.

With his Canadian friend, Iredale, the latter's half-breed, and his own Indian, Tooshalli, the party had set out three weeks ago to find the 'wonderful big moose' the Indians reported were travelling in the Snow River country. They soon found that the tale was true; tracks were abundant; they saw fine animals nearly every day, but though carrying good heads, the hunters expected better still and left them alone. Pushing up the river to a chain of small lakes near its source, they then separated into two parties, each with its nine-foot bark canoe, and packed in for three days after the yet bigger animals the Indians agreed would be found in the deeper woods beyond. Excitement was keen, expectation keener still. The day before they separated, Iredale shot the biggest moose of his life, and its head, bigger even than the grand Alaskan heads, hangs in his house today. Grimwood's hunting blood was fairly up. His blood was of the fiery, not to say ferocious, quality. It almost seemed he liked killing for its own sake.

Four days after the party broke into two he came upon a gigantic track, whose measurements and length of stride keyed every nerve he possessed to its highest tension.

Tooshalli examined the tracks for some minutes with care. 'It is the biggest moose in the world,' he said at length, a new expression on his inscrutable red visage.

Following it all that day, they yet got no sight of the big fellow that seemed to be frequenting a little marshy dip of country, too small to be called valley, where willow and undergrowth abounded. He had not yet scented his pursuers. They were after him again at dawn. Towards the evening of the second day Grimwood caught a sudden glimpse of the monster among a thick clump of willows, and the sight of the magnificent head that easily beat all records set his heart beating like a hammer with excitement. He aimed and fired. But the moose, instead of crashing, went thundering away through the farther scrub and disappeared, the sound of his plunging canter presently dying away. Grimwood had missed, even if he had wounded.

They camped, and all next day, leaving the canoe behind, they followed the huge track, but though finding signs of blood, these were not plentiful, and the shot had evidently only grazed the animal.. The travelling was of the hardest. Towards evening, utterly exhausted, the spoor led them to the ridge they now stood upon, gazing down into the enchanting valley that opened at their feet. The giant moose had gone down into this valley. He would consider himself safe there. Greenwood agreed with the Indian's judgement. They would camp for the night and continue at dawn the wild hunt after 'the biggest moose in the world.'

Supper was over, the small fire used for cooking dying down, when Grimwood became first aware that the Indian was not behaving quite as usual. What particular detail drew his attention is hard to say. He was a slow-witted, heavy man, full-blooded, unobservant; a fact had to hurt him through his comfort, through his pleasure, before he noticed it. Yet anyone else must have observed the changed mood of the Redskin long ago. Tooshalli had made the fire, fried the bacon, served the tea, and was arranging the blankets, his own and his employer's, before the latter remarked upon his — silence. Tooshalli had not uttered a word for over an hour and a half, since he had first set eyes upon the new valley, to be exact. And his employer now noticed the unaccustomed silence, because after food he liked to listen to wood talk and hunting lore.

'Tired out, aren't you?' said big Grimwood, looking into the dark face across the firelight. He resented the absence of conversation, now that he noticed it. He was over-weary himself, he felt more irritable than usual, though his temper was always vile.

'Lost your tongue, eh?' he went on with a growl, as the Indian returned his stare with solemn, expressionless face. That dark inscrutable look got on his nerves a bit. 'Speak up, man!' he exclaimed sharply. 'What's it all about?'

The Englishman had at last realised that there was something to 'speak up' about. The discovery, in his present state, annoyed him further. Tooshalli stared gravely, but made no reply. The silence was prolonged almost into minutes. Presently the head turned sideways, as though the man listened. The other watched him very closely, anger growing in him.

But it was the way the Redskin turned his head, keeping his body rigid, that gave the jerk to Grimwood's nerves, providing him with a sensation he had never known in his life before — it gave him what is generally called 'the goose-flesh.' It seemed to jangle his entire system, yet at the same time made him cautious. He did not like it, this combination of emotions puzzled him.

'Say something, I tell you,' he repeated in a harsher tone,

108

raising his voice. He sat up, drawing his great body closer to the fire. 'Say something, damn it!'

His voice fell dead against the surrounding trees, making the silence of the forest unpleasantly noticeable. Very still the great woods stood about them; there was no wind, no stir of branches; only the crackle of a snapping twig was audible from time to time, as the night-life moved unwarily sometimes, watching the humans round their little fire. The October air had a frosty touch that nipped.

The Redskin did not answer. No muscle of his neck nor of his stiffened body moved. He seemed all ears.

'Well?' repeated the Englishman, lowering his voice this time instinctively. 'What d'you hear, God damn it!' The touch of odd nervousness that made his anger grow betrayed itself in his language.

Tooshalli slowly turned his head back again to its normal position, the body rigid as before.

'I hear nothing, Mr Grimwood,' he said, gazing with quiet dignity into his employer's eyes.

This was too much for the other, a man of savage temper at the best of times. He was the type of Englishman who held strong views as to the right way of treating 'inferior' races.

'That's a lie, Tooshalli, and I won't have you lie to me. Now what was it? Tell me at once!'

'I hear nothing,' repeated the other. 'I only think.'

'And what is it you're pleased to think?' Impatience made a nasty expression round the mouth.

'I go not,' was the abrupt reply, unalterable decision in the voice.

The man's rejoinder was so unexpected that Grimwood found nothing to say at first. For a moment he did not take its meaning; his mind, always slow, was confused by impatience, also by what he considered the foolishness of the little scene. Then in a flash he understood; but he also understood the immovable obstinacy of the race he had to deal with. Tooshalli was informing him that he refused to go into the valley where the big moose had vanished. And his astonishment was so great at first that he merely sat and stared. No words came to him.

'It is —' said the Indian, but used a native term.

'What's that mean?' Grimwood found his tongue, but his quiet tone was ominous.

'Mr Grimwood, it means the "Valley of the Beasts",' was the reply in a tone quieter still.

The Englishman made a great, a genuine effort at self-control. He was dealing, he forced himself to remember, with a superstitious Redskin. He knew the stubbornness of the type. If the man left him his sport was irretrievably spoilt, for he could not hunt in this wilderness alone, and even if he got the coveted head, he could never, never get it out alone. His native selfishness seconded his effort. Persuasion, if only he could keep back his rising anger, was his role to play.

'The Valley of the Beasts,' he said, a smile on his lips rather than in his darkening eyes; 'but that's just what we want. It's beasts we're after, isn't it?' His voice had a false cheery ring that could not have deceived a child. 'But what d'you mean, anyhow – the Valley of the Beasts?' He asked it with a dull attempt at sympathy.

'It belong to Ishtot, Mr Grimwood.' The man looked him full in the face, no flinching in the eyes.

'My – our – big moose is there,' said the other, who recognised the name of the Indian Hunting God, and understanding better, felt confident he would soon persuade his man. Tooshalli, he remembered, too, was nominally a Christian. 'We'll follow him at dawn and get the biggest head the world has ever seen. You will be famous,' he added, his temper better in hand again. 'Your tribe will honour you. And the white hunters will pay you much money.'

'He go there to save himself. I go not.'

The other's anger revived with a leap at this stupid obstinacy. But, in spite of it, he noticed the odd choice of words. He began to realise that nothing now would move the man. At the same time he also realised that violence on his part must prove worse than useless. Yet violence was natural to his 'dominant' type. 'That brute Grimwood' was the way most men spoke of him.

'Back at the settlement you're a Christian, remember,' he tried, in his clumsy way, another line. 'And disobedience means hellfire. You know that!'

'I a Christian — at the post,' was the reply, 'but out here the Red God rule. Ishtot keep that valley for himself. No Indian hunt there.' It was as though a granite boulder spoke.

The savage temper of the Englishman, enforced by the long difficult suppression, rose wickedly into sudden flame. He stood up, kicking his blankets aside. He strode across the dying fire to the Indian's side. Tooshalli also rose. They faced each other, two humans alone in the wilderness, watched by countless invisible forest eyes.

Tooshalli stood motionless, yet as though he expected violence from the foolish, ignorant white-face. 'You go alone, Mr Grimwood.' There was no fear in him.

Grimwood choked with rage. His words came forth with difficulty, though he roared them into the silence of the forest:

'I pay you, don't I? You'll do what *I* say, not what *you* say!' His voice woke the echoes.

The Indian, arms hanging by his side, gave the old reply.

'I go not,' he repeated firmly.

It stung the other into uncontrollable fury.

The beast then came uppermost; it came out. 'You've said that once too often, Tooshalli!' and he struck him brutally in the face. The Indian fell, rose to his knees again, collapsed sideways beside the fire, then struggled back into a sitting position. He never once took his eyes from the white man's face.

Beside himself with anger, Grimwood stood over him. 'Is that enough? Will you obey me now?' he shouted.

'I go not,' came the thick reply, blood streaming from his mouth. The eyes had no flinching in them. 'That valley Ishtot keep. Ishtot see us now. *He see you.*' The last words he uttered with strange, almost uncanny emphasis.

Grimwood, arm raised, fist clenched, about to repeat his terrible assault, paused suddenly. His arm sank to his side. What exactly stopped him he could never say. For one thing, he feared his own anger, feared that if he let himself go he would not stop till he had killed — committed murder. He knew his own fearful temper and stood afraid of it. Yet it was not only that. The calm firmness of the Redskin, his courage under pain, and something in the fixed and burning eyes arrested him. Was it also something in the words he had used – 'Ishtot see *you*' – that stung him into a queer caution midway in his violence?

He could not say. He only knew that a momentary sense of awe came over him. He became unpleasantly aware of the enveloping forest, so still, listening in a kind of impenetrable, remorseless silence. This lonely wilderness, looking silently upon what might easily prove murder, laid a faint, inexplicable chill upon his raging blood. The hand dropped slowly to his side again, the fist unclenched itself, his breath came more evenly.

'Look you here,' he said, adopting without knowing it the local way of speech. 'I ain't a bad man, though your going-on do make a man damned tired. I'll give you another chance.' His voice was sullen, but a new note in it surprised even himself. 'I'll do that. You can have the night to think it over, Tooshalli – see? Talk it over with your —'

He did not finish the sentence. Somehow the name of the Redskin God refused to pass his lips. He turned away, flung himself into his blankets, and in less than ten minutes, exhausted as much by his anger as by the day's hard going, he was sound asleep.

The Indian, crouching beside the dying fire, had said nothing.

Night held the woods, the sky was thick with stars, the life of the forest went about its business quietly, with that wondrous skill which millions of years have perfected. The Redskin, so close to this skill that he instinctively used and borrowed from it, was silent, alert and wise, his outline as inconspicuous as though he merged, like his four-footed teachers, into the mass of the surrounding bush.

He moved perhaps, yet nothing knew he moved. His wisdom, derived from that eternal, ancient mother who from infinite experience makes no mistakes, did not fail him. His soft tread made no sound; his breathing, as his weight, was calculated. The stars observed him, but they did not tell; the light air knew his whereabouts, yet without betrayal. . . .

The chill dawn gleamed at length between the trees, lighting the pale ashes of an extinguished fire, also of a bulky, obvious form beneath a blanket. The form moved clumsily. The cold was penetrating.

And that bulky form now moved because a dream had come to trouble it. A dark figure stole across its confused field of vision. The form started, but it did not wake. The figure spoke: 'Take this,' it whispered, handing a little stick, curiously carved. 'It is the totem of great Ishtot. In the valley all memory of the White Gods will leave you. Call upon Ishtot. ... Call on Him if you dare'; and the dark figure glided away out of the dream and out of all remembrance. ...

2

The first thing Grimwood noticed when he woke was that Tooshalli was not there. No fire burned, no tea was ready. He felt exceedingly annoyed. He glared about him, then got up with a curse to make the fire. His mind seemed confused and troubled. At first he only realised one thing clearly – his guide had left him in the night.

It was very cold. He lit the wood with difficulty and made his tea, and the actual world came gradually back to him. The Red Indian had gone; perhaps the blow, perhaps the superstitious terror, perhaps both, had driven him away. He was alone, that was the outstanding fact. For anything beyond outstanding facts, Grimwood felt little interest. Imaginative speculation was beyond his compass. Close to the brute creation, it seemed, his nature lay.

It was while packing his blankets – he did it automatically, a dull, vicious resentment in him – that his fingers struck a bit of wood that he was about to throw away when its unusual shape caught his attention suddenly. His odd dream came back then. But was it a dream? The bit of wood was undoubtedly a totem stick. He examined it. He paid it more attention than he meant to, wished to. Yes, it was unquestionably a totem stick. The dream, then, was not a dream. Tooshalli had quit, but, following with Redskin faithfulness some code of his own, had left him the means of safety. He chuckled sourly, but thrust the stick inside his belt. 'One never knows,' he mumbled to himself.

He faced the situation squarely. He was alone in the

wilderness. His capable, experienced woodsman had deserted him. The situation was serious. What should he do? A weakling would certainly retrace his steps, following the track they had made, afraid to be left alone in this vast hinterland of pathless forest. But Grimwood was of another build. Alarmed he might be, but he would not give in. He had the defects of his own qualities. The brutality of his nature argued force. He was determined and a sportsman. He would go on. And ten minutes after breakfast, having first made a *cache* of what provisions were left over, he was on his way – down across the ridge and into the mysterious valley, the Valley of the Beasts.

It looked, in the morning sunlight, entrancing. The trees closed in behind him, but he did not notice. It led him on. . . .

He followed the track of the gigantic moose he meant to kill, and the sweet, delicious sunshine helped him. The air was like wine, the seductive spoor of the great beast, with here and there a faint splash of blood on leaves or ground, lay for ever just before his eyes. He found the valley, though the actual word did not occur to him, enticing; more and more he noticed the beauty, the desolate grandeur of the mighty spruce and hemlock, the splendour of the granite bluffs which in places rose above the forest and caught the sun. . . . The valley was deeper, vaster than he had imagined. He felt safe, at home in it, though, again, these actual terms did not occur to him. . . . Here he could hide for ever and find peace. . . . He became aware of a new quality in the deep loneliness. The scenery for the first time in his life appealed to him, and the form of the appeal was curious – he felt the comfort of it.

For a man of his habit, this was odd, yet the new sensations stole over him so gently, their approach so gradual, that they were first recognised by his consciousness indirectly. They had already established themselves in him before he noticed them; and the indirectness took this form – that the passion of the chase gave place to an interest in the valley itself. The lust of the hunt, the fierce desire to find and kill, the keen wish, in a word, to see his quarry within range, to aim, to fire, to witness the natural consummation of the long expedition – these had all become measurably less, while the effect of the valley upon him had increased in strength. There was a welcome about it that he did not understand.

The change was singular, yet, oddly enough, it did not occur to him as singular; it was unnatural, yet it did not strike him so. To a dull mind of his unobservant, unanalytical type, a change had to be marked and dramatic before he noticed it; something in the nature of a shock must accompany it for him to recognise it had happened. And there had been no shock. The spoor of the great moose was much clearer, now that he caught up with the animal that made it; the blood more frequent; he had noticed the spot where it had rested, its huge body leaving a marked imprint on the soft ground; where it had reached up to eat the leaves of saplings here and there was also visible; he had come undoubtedly very near to it, and any minute now might see its great bulk within range of an easy shot. Yet his ardour had somehow lessened.

He first realised this change in himself when it suddenly occurred to him that the animal itself had grown less cautious. It must scent him easily now, since a moose, its sight being indifferent, depends chiefly for its safety upon its unusually keen sense of smell, and the wind came from behind him. This now struck him as decidedly uncommon: the moose itself was obviously careless of his close approach. It felt no fear.

It was this inexplicable alteration of the animal's behaviour that made him recognise, at last, the alteration in his own. He had followed it now for a couple of hours and had descended some eight hundred to a thousand feet; the trees were thinner and more sparsely placed; there were open, park-like places where silver birch, sumach and maple splashed their blazing colours; and a crystal stream, broken by many waterfalls, foamed past towards the bed of the great valley, yet another thousand feet below. By a quiet pool against some over-arching rocks, the moose had evidently paused to drink, paused at its leisure, moreover. Grimwood, rising from a close examination of the direction the creature had taken after drinking – the hoof-marks were fresh and very distinct in the marshy ground about the pool

– looked suddenly straight into the great creature's eyes. It was not twenty yards from where he stood, yet he had been standing on that spot for at least ten minutes, caught by the wonder and loneliness of the scene. The moose, therefore, had been close beside him all this time. It had been calmly drinking, undisturbed by his presence, unafraid.

The shock came now, the shock that woke his heavy nature into realisation. For some seconds, probably for minutes, he stood rooted to the ground, motionless, hardly breathing. He stared as though he saw a vision. The animal's head was lowered, but turned obliquely somewhat, so that the eyes, placed sideways in its great head, could see him properly; its immense proboscis hung as though stuffed upon an English wall; he saw the fore-feet planted wide apart, the slope of the enormous shoulders dropping back towards the fine hind-quarters and lean flanks. It was a magnificent bull. The horns and head justified his wildest expectations, they were superb, a record specimen, and a phrase – where had he heard it? – ran vaguely, as from far distance, through his mind: 'The biggest moose in the world.'

There was the extraordinary fact, however, that he did not shoot; nor feel the wish to shoot. The familiar instinct, so strong hitherto in his blood, made no sign; the desire to kill apparently had left him. To raise his rifle, aim and fire had become suddenly an absolute impossibility.

He did not move. The animal and the human stared into each other's eyes for a length of time whose interval he could not measure. Then came a soft noise close beside him: the rifle had slipped from his grasp and fallen with a thud into the mossy earth at his feet. And the moose, for the first time now, was moving. With slow, easy stride, its great weight causing a squelching sound as the feet drew out of the moist ground, it came towards him, the bulk of the shoulders giving it an appearance of swaying like a ship at sea. It reached his side, is almost touched him, the magnificent head bent low, the spread of the gigantic horns lay beneath his very eyes. He could have patted, stroked it. He saw, with a touch of pity, that blood trickled from a sore in its left shoulder, matting the thick hair. It sniffed the fallen rifle.

Then, lifting its head and shoulders again, it sniffed the air, this time with an audible sound that shook from Grimwood's mind the last possibility that he witnessed a vision or dreamed a dream. One moment it gazed into his face, its big brown eyes shining and unafraid, then turned abruptly, and swung away at a speed ever rapidly increasing across the park-like spaces till it was lost finally in the dark tangle of undergrowth beyond. And the Englishman's muscles turned to paper, his paralysis passed, his legs refused to support his weight, and he sank heavily to the ground.

3

IT SEEMS he slept, slept long and heavily; he sat up, stretched himself, yawned and rubbed his eyes. The sun had moved across the sky, for the shadows, he saw, now ran from west to east, and they were long shadows. He had slept evidently for hours, and evening was drawing in. He was aware that he felt hungry. In his pouch-like pockets he had dried meat, sugar, matches, tea, and the little billy that never left him. He would make a fire, boil some tea and eat.

But he took no steps to carry out his purpose, he felt disinclined to move, he sat thinking, thinking. . . . What was he thinking about? He did not know, he could not say exactly; it was more like fugitive pictures that passed across his mind. Who, and where, was he! This was the Valley of the Beasts, that he knew; he felt sure of nothing else. How long had he been here, and where had he come from, and why? The questions did not linger for their answers, almost as though his interest in them was merely automatic. He felt happy, peaceful, unafraid.

He looked about him, and the spell of this virgin forest came upon him like a charm; only the sound of falling water, the murmur of wind sighing among innumerable branches, broke the enveloping silence. Overhead, beyond the crests of the towering trees, a cloudless evening sky was paling into transparent orange, opal, mother of pearl. He saw buzzards soaring lazily. A scarlet tanager flashed by. Soon would the owls begin to call and the darkness fall like a sweet black veil and hide all detail, while the stars sparkled in their countless thousands. . . .

A glint of something that shone upon the ground caught his eye – a smooth, polished strip of rounded metal: his rifle. And he started to his feet impulsively, yet not knowing exactly what he meant to do. At the sight of the weapon, something had leaped to life in him, then faded out, died down, and was gone again.

'I'm – I'm —' he began muttering to himself, but could not finish what he was about to say. His name had disappeared completely. 'I'm in the Valley of the Beasts,' he repeated in place of what he sought but could not find.

This fact, that he was in the Valley of the Beasts, seemed the only positive item of knowledge that he had. About the name something known and familiar clung, though the sequence that led up to it he could not trace. Presently, nevertheless, he rose to his feet, advanced a few steps, stooped and picked up the shining metal thing, his rifle. He examined it a moment, a feeling of dread and loathing rising in him, a sensation of almost horror that made him tremble, then, with a convulsive movement that betrayed an intense reaction of some sort he could not comprehend, he flung the thing far from him into the foaming torrent. He saw the splash it made, he also saw that same instant a large grizzly bear swing heavily along the bank not a dozen yards from where he stood. It, too, heard the splash, for it started, turned, paused a second, then changed its direction and came towards him. It came up close. Its fur brushed his body. It examined him leisurely, as the moose had done, sniffed, half rose upon its terrible hind legs, opened its mouth so that red tongue and gleaming teeth were plainly visible, then flopped back upon all fours again with a deep growling that yet had no anger in it, and swung off at a quick trot back to the bank of the torrent. He had felt its hot breath upon his face, but he had felt no fear. The monster was puzzled but not hostile. It disappeared.

'They know not —' he sought for the word 'man', but could not find it. 'They have never been hunted.'

The words ran through his mind, if perhaps he was not entirely certain of their meaning; they rose, as it were, automatically; a familiar sound lay in them somewhere. At the same time there rose feelings in him that were equally, though in another way, familiar and quite natural, feelings he had once known intimately but long since laid aside.

What were they? What was their origin? They seemed distant as the stars, yet were actually in his body, in his blood and nerves, part and parcel of his flesh. Long, long ago. . . . Oh, how long, how long?

Thinking was difficult; feeling was what he most easily and naturally managed. He could not think for long; feeling rose up and drowned the effort quickly.

That huge and awful bear -- not a nerve, not a muscle quivered in him as its acrid smell rose to his nostrils, its fur brushed down his legs. Yet he was aware that somewhere there was danger, though not here. Somewhere there was attack, hostility, wicked and calculated plans against him -- as against that splendid, roaming animal that had sniffed, examined, then gone its own way, satisfied. Yes, active attack, hostility and careful, cruel plans against his safety, but -- not here. Here he was safe, secure, at peace; here he was happy; here he could roam at will, no eye cast sideways into forest depths, no ear pricked high to catch sounds not explained, no nostrils quivering to scent alarm. He felt this, but he did not think it. He felt hungry, thirsty too.

Something prompted him now at last to act. His billy lay at his feet, and he picked it up; the matches -- he carried them in a metal case whose screw top kept out all moisture -- were in his hand. Gathering a few dry twigs, he stooped to light them, then suddenly drew back with the first touch of fear he had yet known.

Fire! What *was* fire? The idea was repugnant to him, it was impossible, he was afraid of fire. He flung the metal case after the rifle and saw it gleam in the last rays of sunset, then sink with a little splash beneath the water. Glancing down at his billy, he realised next that he could not make use of it either, nor of the dark dry dusty stuff he had meant to boil in water. He felt no repugnance, certainly no fear, in connection with these things, only he could not handle them, he did not need them, he had forgotten, yes, 'forgotten', what they meant exactly. This strange forgetfulness was increasing in him rapidly, becoming more and more complete with every minute. Yet his thirst must be quenched.

The next moment he found himself at the water's edge; he stooped to fill his billy; paused, hesitated, examined the rushing water, then abruptly moved a few feet higher up the stream, leaving the metal can behind him. His handling of it had been oddly clumsy, his gestures awkward, even unnatural. He now flung himself down with an easy, simple motion of his entire body, lowered his face to a quiet pool he had found, and drank his fill of the cool, refreshing liquid. But, though unaware of the fact, he did not drink. He lapped.

Then, crouching where he was, he ate the meat and sugar from his pockets, lapped more water, moved back a short distance again into the dry ground beneath the trees, but moved this time without rising to his feet, curled his body into a comfortable position and closed his eyes again to sleep. ... No single question now raised its head in him. He felt contentment, satisfaction only. ...

He stirred, shook himself, opened half an eye and saw, as he had felt already in slumber, that he was not alone. In the park-like spaces in front of him, as in the shadowed fringe of the trees at his back, there was sound and movement, the sound of stealthy feet, the movement of innumerable dark bodies. There was the pad and tread of animals, the stir of backs, of smooth and shaggy beasts, in countless numbers. Upon this host fell the light of a half moon sailing high in a cloudless sky; the gleam of stars, sparkling in the clear night air like diamonds, shone reflected in hundreds of ever-shifting eyes, most of them but a few feet above the ground. The whole valley was alive.

He sat upon his haunches, staring, staring, but staring in wonder, not in fear, though the foremost of the great host were so near that he could have stretched an arm and touched them. It was an ever-moving, ever-shifting throng he gazed at, spell-bound, in the pale light of moon and stars, now fading slowly towards the approaching dawn. And the smell of the forest itself was not sweeter to him in that moment than the mingled perfume, raw, pungent, acrid, of this furry host of beautiful wild animals that moved like a sea, with a strange murmuring, too, like sea, as the myriad feet and bodies passed to and fro together. Nor was the gleam of the starry, phosphorescent eyes less pleasantly friendly than those happy lamps that light home-lost wanderers to cosy rooms and safety. Through the wild army, in a word, poured to him the deep comfort of the entire valley, a comfort which held both the sweetness of invitation and the welcome of some magical home-coming.

No thoughts came to him, but feeling rose in a tide of wonder and acceptance. He was in his rightful place. His nature had come home. There was this dim, vague consciousness in him that after long, futile straying in another place where uncongenial conditions had forced him to be unnatural and therefore terrible, he had returned at last where he belonged. Here, in the Valley of the Beasts, he had found peace, security and happiness. He would be – he was at last – himself.

It was a marvellous, even a magical, scene he watched, his nerves at highest tension yet quite steady, his senses exquisitely alert, yet no uneasiness in the full, accurate reports they furnished. Strong as some deep floodtide, yet dim, as with untold time and distance, rose over him the spell of long-forgotten memory of a state where he was content and happy, where he was natural. The outlines, as it were, of mighty, primitive pictures, flashed before him, yet were gone again before the detail was filled in.

He watched the great army of the animals, they were all about him now; he crouched upon his haunches in the centre of an ever-moving circle of wild forest life. Great timber wolves he saw pass to and fro, loping past him with long stride and graceful swing; their red tongues lolling out; they swarmed in hundreds. Behind, yet mingling freely with them, rolled the huge grizzlies, not clumsy as their uncouth bodies promised, but swiftly, lightly, easily, their half tumbling gait masking agility and speed. They gambolled, sometimes they rose and stood half upright, they were comely in their mass and power, they rolled past him so close that he could touch them. And the black bear and the brown went with them, bears beyond counting, monsters and little ones, a splendid multitude. Beyond them, yet only a little farther back, where the park-like spaces made free movement easier, rose a sea of horns and antlers like a miniature forest in the silvery moonlight. The immense tribe of deer gathered in vast throngs beneath the starlit sky. Moose and caribou, he saw, the mighty wapiti, and the smaller deer in their crowding thousands. He heard the sound of meeting horns, the tread of innumerable hoofs, the occasional pawing of the ground as the bigger creatures manoeuvred for more space about them. A wolf, he saw, was licking gently at the shoulder of a great bull-moose that had been injured. And the tide receded, advanced again, once more receded, rising and falling like a living sea whose waves were animal shapes, the inhabitants of the Valley of the Beasts.

Beneath the quiet moonlight they swayed to and fro before him. They watched him, knew him, recognised him. They made him welcome.

He was aware, moreover, of a world of smaller life that formed an under-sea, as it were, numerous under-currents rather, running in and out between the great upright legs of the larger creatures. These, though he could not see them clearly, covered the earth, he was aware, in enormous numbers, darting hither and thither, now hiding, now reappearing, too intent upon their busy purposes to pay him attention like their huger comrades, yet ever and anon tumbling against his back, cannoning from his sides, scampering across his legs even, then gone again with a scuttering sound of rapid little feet, and rushing back into the general host beyond. And with this smaller world also he felt at home.

How long he sat gazing, happy in himself, secure, satisfied, contented, natural, he could not say, but it was long enough for the desire to mingle with what he saw, to know closer contact, to become one with them all — long enough for this deep blind desire to assert itself, so that at length he began to move from his mossy seat towards them, to move, moreover, as they moved, and not upright on two feet.

The moon was lower now, just sinking behind a towering cedar whose ragged crest broke its light into silvery spray. The stars were a little paler too. A line of faint red was visible beyond the heights at the valley's eastern end.

He paused and looked about him, as he advanced slowly, aware that the host already made an opening in their ranks and that the bear even nosed the earth in front, as though to show the way that was easiest for him to follow. Then, suddenly, a lynx leaped past him into the low branches of a hemlock, and he lifted his head to admire its perfect poise. He saw in the same instant the arrival of the birds, the army of the eagles, hawks and buzzards, bird of prey – the awakening flight that just precedes the dawn. He saw the flocks and streaming lines, hiding the whitening stars a moment as they passed with a prodigious whirr of wings. There came the hooting of an owl from the tree immediately overhead where the lynx now crouched, but not maliciously, along its branch.

He started. He half rose to an upright position. He knew not why he did so, knew not exactly why he started. But in the attempt to find his new, and, as it now seemed, his un-accustomed balance, one hand fell against his side and came in contact with a hard straight thing that projected awk-wardly from his clothing. He pulled it out, feeling it all over with his fingers. It was a little stick. He raised it nearer to his eyes, examined it in the light of dawn now growing swiftly, remembered, or half remembered what it was – and stood stock still.

'The totem stick,' he mumbled to himself, yet audibly, finding his speech, and finding another thing – a glint of peering memory – for the first time since entering the valley.

A shock like fire ran through his body; he straightened himself, aware that a moment before he had been crawling upon his hands and knees; it seemed that something broke in his brain, lifting a veil, flinging a shutter free. And Memory peered dreadfully through the widening gap.

'I'm – I'm Grimwood,' his voice uttered though below his breath. 'Tooshalli's left me. I'm alone. . . .!'

He was aware of a sudden change in the animals sur-rounding him. A big, grey wolf sat three feet away, glaring into his face; at its side an enormous grizzly swayed itself from one foot to the other; behind it, as if looking over its shoulder, loomed a gigantic wapiti, its horns merged in the shadows of the drooping cedar boughs. But the northern dawn was nearer, the sun already close to the horizon. He saw details with sharp distinctness now. The great bear rose, balancing a moment on its massive hind-quarters, then took a step toward him, its front paws spread like arms. Its wicked head lolled horribly, as a huge bull-moose, lowering its horns as if about to charge, came up with a couple of long strides and joined it. A sudden excitement ran quivering over the entire host; the distant ranks moved in a new, unpleasant way; a thousand heads were lifted, ears were pricked, a forest of ugly muzzles pointed up to the wind.

And the Englishman, beside himself suddenly with a sense of ultimate terror that saw no possible escape, stiffened and stood rigid. The horror of his position petrified him. Motionless and silent he faced the awful army of his enemies, while the white light of breaking day added fresh ghastliness to the scene which was the setting for his cruel death in the Valley of the Beasts.

Above him crouched the hideous lynx, ready to spring the instant he sought safety in the tree; above it again, he was aware of a thousand talons of steel, fierce hooked beaks of iron, and the angry beating of prodigious wings.

He reeled, for the grizzly touched his body with its outstretched paw; the wolf crouched just before its deadly spring; in another second he would have been torn to pieces, crushed, devoured, when terror, operating naturally as ever, released the muscles of his throat and tongue. He shouted with what he believed was his last breath on earth. He called aloud in his frenzy. It was a prayer to whatever gods there be, it was an anguished cry for help to heaven.

'Ishtot! Great Ishtot, help me!' his voice rang out, while his hand still clutched the forgotten totem stick.

And the Red Heaven heard him.

Grimwood that same instant was aware of a presence that, but for his terror of the beasts, must have frightened him into sheer unconsciousness. A gigantic Red Indian stood before him. Yet, while the figure rose close in front of him, causing the birds to settle and the wild animals to crouch quietly where they stood, it rose also from a great distance, for it seemed to fill the entire valley with its influence, its power, its amazing majesty. In some way, moreover, that he could not understand, its vast appearance included the actual valley itself with all its trees, its running streams, its open spaces and its rocky bluffs. These marked its outline, as it were, the outline of a superhuman shape. There was a mighty bow, there was a quiver of enormous arrows, there was this Redskin figure to whom they belonged.

Yet the appearance, the outline, the face and figure too — these *were* the valley; and when the voice became audible, it was the valley itself that uttered the appalling words. It was the voice of trees and wind, and of running, falling water that woke the echoes in the Valley of the Beasts, as, in that same moment, the sun topped the ridge and filled the scene, the outline of the majestic figure too, with a flood of dazzling light:

'You have shed blood in this my valley. ... *I will not save* ...!'

The figure melted away into the sunlit forest, merging with the new-born day. But Grimwood saw close against his face the shining teeth, hot fetid breath passed over his cheeks, a power enveloped his whole body as though a mountain crushed him. He closed his eyes. He fell. A sharp, crackling sound passed through his brain, but already unconscious, he did not hear it.

*   *   *

His eyes opened again, and the first thing they took in was — fire. He shrank back instinctively.

'It's all right, old man. We'll bring you round. Nothing to be frightened about.' He saw the face of Iredale looking down into his own. Behind Iredale stood Tooshalli. His face was swollen. Grimwood remembered the blow. The big man began to cry.

'Painful still, is it?' Iredale said sympathetically. 'Here, swallow a little more of this. It'll set you right in no time.'

Grimwood gulped down the spirit. He made a violent effort to control himself, but was unable to keep the tears back. He felt no pain. It was his heart that ached, though why or wherefore, he had no idea.

'I'll all to pieces,' he mumbled, ashamed yet somehow not ashamed. 'My nerves are rotten. What's happened?' There was as yet no memory in him.

'You've been hugged by a bear, old man. But no bones broken. Tooshalli saved you. He fired in the nick of time —

a brave shot, for he might easily have hit you instead of the brute.'

'The other brute,' whispered Grimwood, as the whisky worked in him and memory came slowly back.

'Where are we?' he asked presently, looking about him. He saw a lake, canoes drawn up on the shore, two tents, and figures moving. Iredale explained matters briefly, then left him to sleep a bit. Tooshalli, it appeared, travelling without rest, had reached Iredale's camping ground twenty-four hours after leaving his employer. He found it deserted, Iredale and his Indian being on the hunt. When they returned at nightfall, he had explained his presence in his brief native fashion: 'He struck me and I quit. He hunt now alone in Ishtot's Valley of the Beasts. He is dead, I think. I come to tell you.'

Iredale and his guide, with Tooshalli as leader, started off then and there, but Grimwood had covered a considerable distance, though leaving an easy track to follow. It was the moose tracks and the blood that chiefly guided them. They came up with him suddenly enough – in the grip of an enormous bear.

It was Tooshalli that fired.

*   *   *

The Indian lives now in easy circumstances, all his needs cared for, while Grimwood, his benefactor, but no longer his employer, has given up hunting. He is a quiet, easy-tempered, almost gentle sort of fellow, and people wonder rather why he hasn't married. 'Just the fellow to make a good father,' is what they say; 'so kind, good-natured and affectionate'. Among his pipes, in a glass case over the mantelpiece, hangs a totem stick. He declares it saved his soul, but what he means by the expression he has never quite explained.

Ghost & Horror in Pan

Ira Levin

ROSEMARY'S BABY 25p

'At last I have got my wish. I am ridden by a book that plagues my mind and continues to squeeze my heart with fingers of bone. I swear that *Rosemary's Baby* is the most unnerving story I've read' – KENNETH ALLSOP

'. . . if you read this book in the dead of night, do not be surprised if you feel the urge to keep glancing behind you' – QUEEN

'A darkly brilliant tale of modern deviltry that like James' *The Turn of the Screw*, induces the reader to believe the unbelievable. I believed it and was altogether enthralled'
— TRUMAN CAPOTE

A KISS BEFORE DYING 25p
THIS PERFECT DAY 35p